ONE WAY WITCH

DAW Books proudly presents
the novels of Nnedi Okorafor

WHO FEARS DEATH
THE BOOK OF PHOENIX

NOOR

BINTI: THE COMPLETE TRILOGY
(Binti | Binti: Home | Binti: The Night Masquerade
with *Binti: Sacred Fire)*

The Desert Magician's Duology
SHADOW SPEAKER (Book 1)
LIKE THUNDER (Book 2)

She Who Knows
SHE WHO KNOWS (Book 1)
ONE WAY WITCH (Book 2)

ONE WAY WITCH

BOOK TWO OF SHE WHO KNOWS

NNEDI OKORAFOR

DAW BOOKS
New York

Jacket illustration by Greg Ruth
Jacket design by Jim Tierney
Edited by Betsy Wollheim
DAW Book Collectors No. 1981

DAW Books
An imprint of Astra Publishing House
dawbooks.com
DAW Books and its logo are registered trademarks of
Astra Publishing House

Printed in the United States of America

Library of Congress Cataloging-in-Publication Data

Names: Okorafor, Nnedi, author.
Title: One way witch / Nnedi Okorafor.
Description: First edition. | New York : DAW Books, 2025. |
Series: She Who Knows ; book 2
Identifiers: LCCN 2024058337 (print) | LCCN 2024058338 (ebook) |
ISBN 9780756418977 (hardcover) | ISBN 9780756418984 (ebook)
Subjects: LCGFT: Fantasy fiction. | Novels.
Classification: LCC PS3615.K67 O54 2025(print) |
LCC PS3615.K67 (ebook) | DDC 813/.6--dc23/eng/20241223
LC record available at https://lccn.loc.gov/2024058337
LC ebook record available at https://lccn.loc.gov/2024058338

First edition: April 2025
10 9 8 7 6 5 4 3 2 1

Dedicated to my sisters Ngozi Chijioke Okorafor (1973–2021) and Ifeoma Chinyere Okorafor. The Trinity cannot be broken.

Author's Note

In order to properly go on this next part of the journey, it's imperative to know Najeeba's daughter Onyesonwu's story and the players in that tale. However, Najeeba is not one to stop and catch you up. Najeeba doesn't look back, even as she carries it all forward with her. The She Who Knows trilogy is her voice, her mind, her spirit. So you won't get much rehash for context from Najeeba.

On top of this, I, The Writer, cannot summarize the novel of *Who Fears Death*—not well. It's a story that needs to stretch out. That's why it's a novel. Just as Najeeba speaks her story through this trilogy, Onyesonwu speaks her story through *Who Fears Death*. Onyesonwu tells it all to a journalist who has come to her prison cell before she is to be executed by stoning. It is an oral telling, typed into a laptop, presented as a book. Onyesonwu's story is long, full, naked, and haunted;

it's her whole life. However, for the sake of understanding this She Who Knows novella, *One Way Witch*, which continues *after* Onyesonwu has done what she did, I'll try and throw the bones of *Who Fears Death* here:

For a short time, Najeeba had a good life with her first husband Idris. When they were both twenty years old, Nuru militants attacked their village, killing almost everyone. At the time, Najeeba was out in the desert with a group of women "holding conversation" with Ani. And out there, a special team of Nurus, led by the general and sorcerer Daib, came for them. When Najeeba saw the Nuru militants approaching, she'd looked beyond them, at her village in the distance. It was on fire. She screamed so loudly at the sight that the fullness of her voice left her and from that moment to the time we meet her here, that voice remains nothing but a whisper.

The group of Nuru militants raped every single one of these women.

Daib and his militants were bewitched with a juju Daib concocted that made them especially vicious. The juju also made Daib and his militants and the Okeke women they assaulted especially . . . fertile. Every woman from this group who lived became pregnant from the assaults. This was the intent. Nuru and Okeke culture were both patriarchal. Thus, a child was the child of the father. Daib's plans were to disrupt Okeke bloodlines by forcing Nuru children into them. This was weaponized rape. This was violent genetic warfare.

General Daib specifically raped Najeeba because he sensed the unrealized sorceress in her. Daib believed the resulting child would be his heir. After the assault, Najeeba tried to die. When she didn't, Najeeba stumbled home and found her village destroyed. To her joy, her husband Idris was alive. However, Idris turned his back on her, viewing her ravaged body as corrupted, polluted, dead.

And so Najeeba left him, never looking back. She walked into the desert with every intention of dying. But dying truly was harder to do than she expected. She lived and gave birth to a girl full of life and rage. Najeeba named her Onyesonwu, which meant, "who fears death" in Old Igbo. A power name, a taunt. And as Najeeba's father wished for the goddess Ani to give him revenge for the death of his family by making one of his children a sorcerer, Najeeba wished the same for her child Onyesonwu.

Najeeba's wish was fulfilled, for Onyesonwu not

only grew up to be a fierce sorceress, she left home to seek out her biological father, Daib, and kill him. In seeking to avenge her mother and herself, Onyesonwu did something much greater: She changed the world. She wielded powerful juju to rewrite and undo the Great Book, ending Okeke genocide and Nuru hatred of the Okeke people, as a whole. Onyesonwu ushered in a world where the Nuru and the Okeke live side by side in a sort of uncomfortable confused peace.

The first book of She Who Knows is the story of Najeeba before Onyesonwu. *One Way Witch* continues the story. It is now Najeeba's turn to realize the sorceress in herself, that which (witch?) had been requested by her father so long ago. *One Way Witch* begins before Onyesonwu did what she did (The Before) and then shifts to afterwards (The Now), when the world is changed. These are things to know going in.

However, for the full weight of it, to know General Daib, the sorcerers Aro and Sola, and Onyesonwu's stepfather Fadil (her *true* father, for biology is *not* synonymous with fatherhood) during Onyesonwu's own time, please read *Who Fears Death*. I wrote the She Who Knows novellas with *Who Fears Death* as their foundation and *The Book of Phoenix* as strengthening in the cement.

In this volume, we follow the Student. Finally. Najeeba is smiling. There is only one way this witch can go.

Nnedi

CHAPTER 1

Sometimes, It Is *Not* a Teacher That You Need

From high above, in my kponyungo spirit form, I'd watched my daughter Onyesonwu.

I was the size of four camels, lean and strong like a snake, coiled horns, magnificent jaw and made of wind and fire. With my fiery eyes, I watched her walk into the desert with five others: the boy who loved her so purely he would die for her, the girl who would become her greatest champion, the girl who had just killed her abusive father, the girl who knew my daughter would be a legend, and the boy who was just following that girl. I stopped watching when they were miles away. I couldn't bear to see my Onyesonwu leave the town of Jwahir forever. She was twenty years old, the same age I was when Daib raped me.

I opened my eyes. Now back in my physical body, I understood I was completely alone.

Secrets. I've always kept them. Onyesonwu did not know this part of me. Not for months yet. She already had too much to carry; I didn't want to give her more.

Days before she left, I'd unlocked something. I didn't do it for her. I did it for myself. I'd known she was on the cusp of leaving, that she would soon do that thing she couldn't resist doing. I was watching her more closely than she ever suspected. I know my child. And I was excited for her. And I hoped for her, too. Yes, I hoped she would finally do what she needed so dearly to do: Leave Jwahir and go after the man who'd raped me to create her. She was his downfall. I knew all this in my heart. But I also knew her leaving would destroy me.

I brought her to Jwahir when she was six. Soon after, I met my second husband, the blacksmith Fadil Ogundimu. He was a beautiful strong man who loved both Onyesonwu and me with compassion and ferocity. Again, I was happy for a time. Then Fadil died of a heart attack when Onyesonwu was sixteen. To this day, I wonder if Daib, Onyesonwu's biological father, a powerful sorcerer, the man who'd raped me, somehow facilitated Fadil's heart attack. I will never know. Maybe it doesn't matter. Regardless, Fadil was the greatest thing to ever happen to me and my daughter. And then he died. So I have lost my heart before. Onyesonwu was my spirit. Her leaving was unbearable. And what made it different was that I'd known she would go. Soon.

Nights before she would do the thing that drove her into the desert accompanied by her friends, I walked into the desert. I did not go West, this time; I went East. The night was cool and lit by a near full moon. As I walked, the wind felt good. No one was out this way. Back then, on moonlit nights, there were storytellers in the square. They told bloody tales about the West. So the people out and about gathered in the square.

The way I went was quiet, just the way I needed it to be. By the time the dirt road faded to desert, very few had any reason to come this way, I was beginning to prepare. With each step I took onto the soft sand, I grew more anxious. It had to work. But the fact was, I had not done this in decades. When I left my village to marry my first husband, Idris, I left the kponyungo behind. I buried everything I had manifested on the salt roads with my brothers and father. The knowledge, experience, memories. I'd never told Idris a word about any of it. I'd wanted to become someone new, a normal woman.

I laugh now because trying to be a normal woman in a world where most of your people were slaves was foolish. However, in that pocket of fragile peace, I thought I could live my life. I was so stupid, silly, and naïve. But I tried. In that brief time I was with my husband Idris, I *felt* somewhat normal. We were in love.

I'd left my strange past (including the odd death of my father) behind. I'd left my aloof mother. And then my aloof mother died. My brothers both came to tell me. They had already buried her, had all the ceremonies, met with other family members, mourned her passing. "We didn't think it would be . . . healthy for you to know," they said.

I will never know what they meant by that because I didn't ask, and they didn't offer me any details. All they said was that they found mother at home in the garden she'd always paid others to maintain. They declined spending the night or even meeting Idris. Neither of them would look me in the eye; I remember that.

I was sad for some time, but the mystery of her death and the fact that I'd left home behind so that I could be new protected me. And then, months later, the Nuru came and destroyed my new life. They destroyed my village. Idris hid and survived, but they destroyed him, too. The Nuru general who led it all destroyed me.

Still, I didn't reach for the kponyungo. My daughter came into being, grew up to become a fierce sorceress, and still I did not reach for the kponyungo. But that day, I felt like I was at the end. I walked into the desert, in the opposite direction my daughter would soon walk and never return from. I wasn't afraid to be alone. It wasn't me grieving my dead husband, it was losing my child, my focal point. Onyesonwu held me to this world. Without her, I was nothing. I clung to the weight of her. If only to be there for her if she somehow needed me. And so I walked into the desert to unlock something I'd put away long ago.

I looked for the highest sand dune and scaled it. At the top, the wind whipped my bushy hair about. A stream of sand flowed low around my ankles. I bent down and held a hand in it like one would cup water in a shallow river. I rubbed the sand in my hands like salt and then threw it behind me. I sat down in the sand stream, feeling it begin to collect in the bottom part of my garments. I was wearing the periwinkle garments women wore when they held conversation. I had not worn these in two decades, since that day when I nearly lost my soul.

"Are you still there?" I said in my whispery voice. "It's been a while." I had eaten a hearty meal hours earlier with Onyesonwu. Roasted goat meat, fried plantains, coconut curry soup and palm wine. We had talked into the night about many things, except her training with the sorcerer Aro; we discussed what we knew was coming, and the violence in the West. It had been a nice evening. Both my mind and stomach were full, but to do this, it was best to be empty.

A powerful gust of wind blew. I gasped. Exhaled. Looked to the sky. And then I was flying. That easily. The kponyungo had been waiting. I shot up, leaving my body below, still and relaxed. As I flew, I opened my great mouth and roared so loudly the air around me combusted. "YOOOOOOOOOOOOOOOOOOR-RRRR!!" Great coils and blooms of flame burst, lightning crashed, boomed, zapped, and crunched, glorious explosive forces. I flew higher. I was the great lizard beast made of flames and lightning and wind. I roared

again. I had not heard my voice in two decades. I'd
been so suppressed in my body, in my physical mind.
I flew higher. Faster. Oh it was cathartic. Inside, I
wept. Why had I waited so long? Why had I been
afraid of this? What had happened to me? Where had
I been? After that evening, I became the kponyungo
every day.

I hung on to it. When Onyesonwu left, I hung on
to it more. I considered following her, but I held back.
There was something I knew it was time to do first.
Two women started coming to see to my well-being
the day after Onyesonwu left. The Ada was the town
priestess and the wife of the sorcerer Aro; she was one
of the most highly respected woman in Jwahir. Nana
the Wise was nearly 100 years old and an Osugbo
Elder, which made her the most powerful woman in
Jwahir.

My daughter had left because she'd done something Jwahir wouldn't forgive. In a rage, right in the
middle of town square, she'd used juju to force people
there to experience all that had happened to me and
the other women that day. Eyes unable to turn away
from mass rape and murder. Onyesonwu wanted
them all to feel the sense of urgency she felt for the
Okeke people in the West. It was a terrible thing she

did. There were children in the town square that day. And now I wondered if Nana the Wise and the Ada were here just to make sure I didn't do anything as destructive as what Onyesonwu had done.

I waited until my daughter had been gone for five days. The Ada and Nana the Wise wanted to stay over this night. They must have sensed something. But I insisted that I was fine by myself. "Come and stay with me in six days," I told them. And in this way, I became the kponyungo and left my body for the first time in the safety of my home. I sat in the living room, the portrait of Njeri, my husband Fadil's first wife, staring at me. On the floor with my long legs crossed. I wore loose colorful clothing. I made sure one of the windows was open, so the air would remain fresh. Then I closed my eyes. I flew away. And I was gone the entire night.

When I was on the salt roads, I was never gone for more than two hours. Now, I was free. I was alone. During these days of renewal, I never flew west. I went east. Many times, I flew up, toward the stars. Then on the sixth day, before the Ada and Nana the Wise came to stay with me, I went to see the sorcerer named Aro.

━━━

Aro was the Osugbo Elder and great sorcerer who became Onyesonwu's teacher. She only had to nearly kill him first. I would come to understand how it came to that; he is a hard-headed man. He was the one who ushered her to the path of her destiny. I was aware of their fraught teacher-student relationship, though I did not know the fine details. It was not my place to know that part of it. But I also knew Aro in a capacity outside of my daughter's world. You could not be who I am and have no encounter with a man like him in such a small town. By the time my daughter left, he had locked in on me and I on him. He could probably smell me, sense what I was doing.

During those five days alone, once on my way back to my body, a vulture flew beside me for some miles. I slowed so the vulture could keep up. I often flew with birds, usually hawks, owls, and eagles. They could see me, and they didn't fear me. I think they enjoyed the warm air currents I gave off. I'd once had three hawks fly with me for miles, spiraling around me playfully. One had even flown right above my body, and my flames didn't harm it. But this day, the vulture flew beside me and I'd glanced and caught its gaze. What I saw in its eye startled me.

It was not the knowing eye of a great bird. Have you ever known someone so well that even when veiled, all you had to see was a glint of their eye to know it was them? Maybe it is your father's eye or your mother's or best friend's or worst enemy's. You just know it when you see it; that is how strong the connection is. Well, I recognized Aro *immediately*. I *knew* it was him. And I knew that he was not the same as me. Where I had come out of my flesh to become the kponyungo, he had changed his flesh to be a vulture.

I roared at him and he made a raspy, drawn-out hiss and a grunt. This startled me so much that I lost my sense of direction for a minute and flew upward. I righted myself and this must have been enough for him because he banked to the left and flew off.

It was time to go see him. I walked to his hut on foot. I never felt more alone than I did on that walk. I'd awakened in an empty house. My daughter was far away and moving farther by the day. My parents were long dead. My brothers, I didn't know if they were alive and I did not think about them. My first husband Idris was dead to me. My second husband, my beloved Fadil was truly dead. What did I have now? I had what I was walking toward. So I walked, carrying the weight of my reality. With each step, more tears fell from my eyes. My vision blurred and still I walked. I was forty years old.

It was a hot morning, no longer a time of rest. Everything in the dry forest was singing, screaming, calling, responding. The trees sounded weighed down with active insects, birds, spiders, rodents. I knew the way. I'd been here just before Onyesonwu left. I was here for me today.

When I arrived at the cactuses in front of his hut, I paused and looked at them. When I had come here before, I had not gone past these. He'd been waiting for me where I stood and here we had talked. I stepped onto the path to his hut and then took another step. Onyesonwu had mentioned these cactuses, saying that each time she walked past them, they scratched her. I paused and looked at one of them. It was taller than me, wider than me, a lush green, unlike the dull green of most cactuses. I glared at it and said, "Don't. I am a grown woman. I don't care how old you are. I'm here to see Aro; you will respect me."

The cactus stayed a cactus, and I walked on. There were fourteen in all, seven on my left and seven on my right. As I walked past them, I glared at each, daring them. I didn't know what I'd do if one swiped at me, but I would do something. I stopped in the middle, with six behind me and eight before me. Tall hearty plant edifices. I could feel their attention on me. I was reminded of that day at the market when those men realized I was a girl. Aro's hut wasn't far. He wasn't standing before it, but I knew in my gut that he was home. I turned and walked away.

Sometimes, it is *not* a teacher that you need.

———

I returned to the desert that evening. The Ada and Nana the Wise were in my home. I'd heard them coming in, calling my name as I left through the back door. But I wasn't ready to be around anyone yet.

That evening, I did it for the first time; I became the kponyungo and I went *west*. Just a little. And then I flew down to the first town I saw. A refugee town called Banza. It was dark but, for an Okeke town, it was quite awake. There were people walking on the roads, lingering in the shops. The restaurants were noisy with chatter and brightly lit. Many hung around outside. The people here wore tighter fitting colorful garments. This town was not far for me as the kponyungo, but it was for one on foot. Onyesonwu and her friends wouldn't have gotten half this distance, yet already it was so different from Jwahir.

I flew back out into the desert. I was flame and light and it was the dead of night. I wasn't sure how clearly people would see me, nor *what* they would see. I flew down, and there I hovered for a while, inspecting the effects of my kponyungo body on the sand. I must have stayed there for an hour. And below me, the sand had begun to melt into glass. I was ethereal, but I was also there.

I looked up at the night sky. The vastness had always made me feel so specific. In all those planets and stars, there was nothing like me, no one like me. A woman who could do what I could do, who had a sorceress daughter, who'd loved and been loved by a kind talented blacksmith, who'd survived, who'd let go. As I thought about myself, something happened and when it happened, it made so much sense that I laughed. I gently lowered to the molten sand that was cooling to glass. I paused noticing that I was no longer the large lizard-like shape of the kponyungo, but my human form.

My bare feet cracked the glass and then it began to bubble. I wore loose flowing periwinkle garments that blew and shifted as if there was wind. I looked at my hands. I was still spirit, yet I had the callouses I'd earned from my hours of gardening. I knelt down and touched the sand with both of my hands. After about a minute, the sand burned to molten glass. When I concentrated, I could slow it down. I stood up straight and looked toward the town of Banza in the distance. I walked.

———

This is not the story of how I helped my daughter.

First I unlocked those things I'd suppressed for decades. The kponyungo, travelling, what was called going "elu," what I secretly called "witching." Then I learned *on top* of this foundation. I taught it all to myself. I did not need a teacher. I did not need to be apprenticed or mentored. I needed to arrive on my own. I learned I could walk amongst others far away as a spirit and I could speak with them. I talked to the people of Banza. I learned to suppress the heat that radiated from me, for a time. Eventually. I learned how to find my daughter. I watched her, but not often. Only once did I go to her, where I appeared to her as the kponyungo and we flew together. I otherwise stayed away. It was too painful, and it was hard not to intervene. And then, when I knew she was close, I preceded her. It was the only way. They would have killed her if I did not create her as a myth first.

No one is a chosen one without others being chosen, too. My daughter needed her mother. Then I stepped back and out of her story so she could do what she had to do. I waited and I couldn't tell anyone I was waiting. How was I to explain that I was waiting for my daughter to change the world and probably die doing it? I ran my cactus candy shop during the day, ignoring the stares of suspicion and distrust, the whispers and gossip. I took long walks at night.

I was at home when it happened, sitting in the living room with the Ada and Nana the Wise. Nana the Wise had brought three jugs of the beer she loved to brew. That early evening, the three of us were drunk and laughing raucously.

"Oh I have one," Nana the Wise was saying. She leaned way back on the couch as she finished off another cup of the delicious beer. "If you could be a man for one day, what is the first thing you would do?"

"Oh, that's easy," the Ada said. She'd had the most cups of beer as usual. She got up, teetered for a second and then brought her hand to her crotch and simulated masturbation. This sent all three of us into gales of screaming laughter. My world was spinning. I hadn't laughed this hard since long before Onye-sonwu had left. She'd been gone for nearly five months now.

"I think I'd go outside with no shirt on," I said in my whispery voice, when I could finally breathe. "Then maybe I'd look for a man to fight."

More laughter. Nana the Wise was laughing so hard that she was wheezing. Still laughing, the Ada quickly jumped up to hug her. "Are you all right?" she asked.

This was when it crushed me. I was laughing and looking at the only two friends I had in the world–the town custodian of girl and woman traditions and one of the town's leaders. Old women. Powerful women. Women who were pivotal in making Jwahir the peaceful comfortable town it was. Far west from all the killing. Nowhere near where I'd come from.

I felt harsh pains in my head. Right between my

temples. Then at the bridge of my nose. Then my left cheek. The back of my head. My chin. My left eye. I gasped from the raw pain of it all. I felt every stone that they threw at my daughter's head in a city so far away from me that the sun was still high. I fell off my chair, holding my head. My head felt wet, parts of it exposed. But it wasn't the pain. No, no, no, the pain was a distant second to the realization.

"Onyesonwu," I softly screamed. I had no voice and never had this fact angered me so deeply. I rolled to my side and started punching the chair in front of me. By this time, the Ada was at my side, Nana the Wise slowly kneeling beside her. But all I could focus on was that my daughter was dying. She was slipping away. As she went, she was still. She was quiet. Onyesonwu was looking somewhere else. She was focused. Because she was calm, I calmed.

She spoke to me. Not in voice, in spirit. So calm. For the first time, my daughter who had been born raging at the world was at peace. "Mama, here I go," she said. There was a moment. Then I burst into tears as I curled in on myself on the floor.

"What is wrong?" Nana the Wise asked. My eyes were squeezed shut, so I couldn't see her face, but she sounded terrified.

"Breathe," the Ada said. She put her hand on my shoulder.

I opened my mouth wide and took a loud, ragged deep breath.

"Now, exhale," she said.

I exhaled. And when I did, I felt it all change. The sensation was like warm water flowing over me. I slowly opened my eyes and I could *see it*. It was like a hallucination. I was looking at the Ada and Nana the Wise, as they crouched over me. They both looked so concerned. The Ada was wearing one of her loose dresses, it was green. Nana the Wise was wearing pants and a matching top made of orange silky material. Neither wore shoes. Nana the Wise had her hair shaven close to her head and she wore her signature bronze hoop earrings. The Ada wore a necklace and bracelets made of braided palm fibers.

Right before my eyes, the Ada's dress became blue and she was now wearing silver bangles, a necklace and several tiny silver hoop earrings that went up her ear. Nana the Wise's orange clothes became white and her hair became long thick grey braids. Then Nana the Wise sprouted brown wings like a giant eagle. They stretched as she leaned in and the Ada moved away from them as if she was used to the wings' being there. Then another waterlike wave passed, and Nana the Wise's wings disappeared.

I inhaled and exhaled again. My head felt better. But even in my bones, I could feel that everything was different. Neither Nana the Wise nor the Ada noticed a thing. They didn't look at their clothes with confusion. Nana the Wise pushed her hair back before helping me up, as if it had always been there. The Ada's signature bronze hoop earrings were gone. Her silver bangles clicked as she took my other shoulder, and she seemed used to their clicking.

Both of them were very worried about me. They couldn't understand what had happened. When I said, "My daughter. I think something happened," they both looked even more worried.

"I think you might have had a little too much beer," Nana the Wise said. They helped me to the couch. Then they both stepped away but I could hear Nana the Wise whisper, "It's making her hallucinate about her baby. Do *you* feel all right? Maybe my beer is bad."

"I feel fine," the Ada said. "And I had twice as much as her."

They helped me dress for bed and then they left. It was interesting. They had been staying at my place to keep me company for weeks. Now, it was as if they'd never done so. I didn't go outside until the morning. I was afraid.

━━━

My daughter Onyesonwu saved the world. She changed it most likely using something the sorcerer Aro taught her. Whatever she did caused the change to wash over the land. The Okeke people and the Nuru people were cured. That is the only way I can describe it. When I went to the market now, though Jwahir was still a proudly Okeke town, you saw some Nuru people at the market. People did business with Nuru travelers. There were old Okeke men who sat on stools and broke kola with old Nuru men near the iroko tree. There were a few Nuru scholars who came to study in the house of Osugbo. I even saw an Okeke Nuru couple walking down the road, arms around each other's waists. I'd paused at this, having many thoughts.

No one remembered the hate. Well, most did not.

I remembered everything. I remembered my daughter. The hate she endured. The hate I and all Okeke people endured. How I'd helped my daughter to achieve the change. I remembered everything, and those around me did not. And this made me feel more alone than ever. I walked around knowing about a horror that never happened, yet happened to me and so many others. I still had the kponyungo. Since I was a teen, that was one thing in my life that had not changed.

I could leave my body and become the fiery beast, and I could fly so so far. I could project myself hundreds of miles away. These were things I'd discovered I could do when I was a teen and now, decades later, was developing. Things that were old and solid had a special significance to me. They had weathered whatever my daughter had done to right all the wrongs.

For months, I kept all this to myself. I had my shop at the market, I participated in town events, I attended get togethers that the Ada organized. She was always introducing me to men because she felt I needed a husband. None were ever good enough. And I spent much time in the desert. Most thought I was just a deeply spiritual woman, that I was one of those who Held Conversation with the goddess Ani often, even when there was no group retreat. I was fine with that, and I even played it up by wearing the periwinkle garments that women wore when they went on group retreats.

Until the day my curiosity got the better of me. I had avoided the West in my travels. But this day I was missing Onyesonwu. I was missing my husband Fadil. The house felt both empty and full. Empty of the loves of my life and full of memories of them. I just wanted to go back. Back to when I was young and mystical, when people looked at me and wondered what was ahead for me, when I had beautiful brothers and beautiful parents. When I had a place in society and it wasn't strange. I just wanted to go back. So for the first time since I left at the age of eighteen, I went back to my village.

It was the dead of night as I flew there. The moon was high. It made me think of the night my father had to leave his own village. Miles folded on miles as I traveled as the kponyungo, a creature of fire in the sky. West. Over so much quiet desert. I flew low in these places, shooting past a small herd of wild camels, a vulture in flight, a snake sidewinding up a dune, stunted gnarled trees, dust. I saw no human travelers. I knew where home was. As the kponyungo, a sense of place is central. I could find any place I could imagine.

I was coming up on it now. The white, square-shaped homes and buildings, dusty roads. Adoro 5 was a little bigger, more a town now than a village. In the distance I could see the Paper House. It still stood. I drew in my brightness, simmering a dull orange, as I flew low. People would see me, but I would not cause distress, just intrigue. At this hour, anyone who was alive assumed enigmatic creatures would be out.

Would my home still be there? Would one of my brothers and his family be living in it? Or would it be abandoned, crumbling to dust. What had my daughter's glorious success done to my first home?

I was low as I approached the road that went into Adoro 5. I knew this road. It was on the East side. There was a large house here owned by a camel seller. I could see the corral where the family kept its most prized camels. Still there. I was dizzy with anticipation. With joy. Home was still home. I was on the wide dirt road now. As expected, no one was on it. It had to be around 3 AM, the dead of night. I made a left. The road toward school. That was when I spotted it. I flew upward. *No*, I thought, growling in my kponyungo voice. I decided to fly back East. Immediately. But first . . . I had to see.

Oh, I saw.

I flew above it and it saw me! It looked up and watched me fly by—A tall figure in dark garments, maybe a man. No, it was not a man at all. Up to now, I had never seen it. No one I knew had ever seen it, except for one of my agemates who'd been taken and returned. Nevertheless, I knew *exactly* what I was seeing. This was the Cleanser, the mysterious being who came every few years and took one of the young people in Adoro villages for one day and brought them back changed. We accepted the Cleanser as we accepted being outcast by belonging to the goddess Adoro. It was a dark blessing. Whoever was taken and returned would always grow up to be special; they were gifted. Or so we believed.

On this night, behind the Cleanser walked a girl of about fifteen with rich dark skin, her hair cropped close to her head, shiny golden hoops dangling from her ears, a deeply worried look on her face.

There was a difference now. I was older. I was wiser. And I was in my kponyungo form. And so as I gazed upon the Cleanser, and though I didn't understand the why or the how, I saw it for what it was. I saw this with such intense clarity that for a moment I was sure my mind would break. I forced myself to look a moment longer, until my understanding was solid.

"All this time," I whispered with despair. "Oh Ani, all this time."

Onyesonwu's sacrifice had not solved all the nastiest problems of our people. We called it "The Cleanser"; clearly not all types of "cleanliness" were good for us.

I fled.

———

I opened my eyes to the darkness of my empty home. My face was wet with tears. Even as I traveled, my body still wept for what I'd learned. I understood what it was that I needed to do now. I had to go back home and kill the Cleanser.

I knew how to approach Aro the sorcerer. My daughter's teacher. He was sitting outside of his hut, facing the desert, thinking whatever the man thought at times like this, when I flew at him as the kponyungo. When he saw me coming, he changed into a vulture and soon we were both flying side by side. We flew over Jwahir. I flew at my slowest, so that he could keep up. I chose a spot at the top of a high sand dune, a half mile outside town. I stood there in my human form, waiting as he circled above. He flew off.

I was spirit, wearing my shifting periwinkle garments that I always manifested when I took this form. I waited longer. And a half hour later, I saw him coming over a sand dune. I'd had no doubt that he could find my exact location. Aro was a powerful sorcerer. And he was going to teach me. At least this was what I had decided.

There was a strong gusty breeze as he walked up to me. His loose tan pants and kaftan swept around him. I smiled, knowing the sandy dust pelted him but didn't touch me because there was no flesh to touch. It didn't seem to bother him, though.

"You have decided to come to me, Najeeba," he said, his arms across his chest as he walked right up to me.

"I have."

"Why?"

"I have things to learn."

He paused, looking me up and down. "You seem to know enough."

"I want to be a sorcerer."

"Sorceress."

"Sorcerer," I pressed.

"Do you even know what it is that you can do? What it's called?"

"I have begun to call it 'witching,'" I said. I'd never really had the nerve to name my abilities when I was a teen. Now, many decades later, it felt right to name it.

"It's called going elu," Aro said. "The word is old, it means 'sky.' Going elu is not common nor is it an easy thing." He paused to look at me. Then he frowned and muttered, "Something is wrong with the women in your bloodline."

"Women?" I asked. "So you remember?"

"I do." He paused, realizing that I did, too. "Maybe those who . . . loved her remember."

We looked at each other for a long time, and then I said it: "I have not met anyone else who remembers."

He nodded. "Not even the girl Diti and her husband Fanasi remember any more."

The two who had been with Onyesonwu and then returned to Jwahir weeks later hadn't told me much and I hadn't asked them much. They'd been skittish and secretive when I'd gone to see them. All I really got from them was that Onyesonwu and the others were alive and determined, except for Binta who'd been killed in some backward village defending my daughter. Diti had begun to cry and that was that. It wasn't long after talking to those two that I knew I would find a way to use my abilities to seek out my daughter my way.

"Onyesonwu was not easy for common people to love," I said.

"No," Aro said.

"Remembering is painful."

"I prefer it." He paused again, now frowning at me. "Let's walk."

We headed toward to Jwahir.

"I rather like your soft voice," Aro said snidely. "Even powerful women are better off when mostly quiet."

I snarled with annoyance. "Have you not learned anything from my daughter?"

He chuckled.

When we were close to the city limits we stopped. This place was used as a refugee camp for those who'd fled the West. When my daughter and I had first arrived in Jwahir, this was where we'd stayed for some months. It was gone now, replaced with a field of corn irrigated by a series of strategically placed capture stations. The green of the lush stalks as they waved in the breeze was jarring.

"I haven't been out this way since things changed," I said. "I usually fly east."

"That is understandable. The day it happened, I flew all around Jwahir. The changes are beautiful. Your daughter saved the world and few will ever know it."

Tears welled in my eyes. "My heart hurts."

He nodded. "Return to your body. Meet me at my hut. In the back."

I changed and flew off. As the kponyungo, I burned bright, flying low, hoping people below saw me and wondered. I hoped a few fretted. And I hoped a few cried. They all benefited from my daughter's sacrifice yet they'd all driven her away in the first place because she showed them the truth. I burned brighter. When I returned to myself sitting in my living room, I opened my eyes, feeling calmer, though still a bit angry.

I went to the kitchen and grabbed a handful of groundnuts. I ate them as I walked to Aro's hut. I wore a light but long blue dress and sandals, and I wore my long grey-brown braids down. I passed several people on my way, a group of brightly dressed chattery teenagers, some women I knew who were on their way to the market, a crew of workers building a house, several people riding scooters. When I left the busy main road, turning onto the narrow path to

Aro's hut, I was relieved. The path was calm, quiet and mysterious; I could think here. The dry forest was so strikingly different from what was behind me, it could have been its own realm. And this wasn't that far from the truth because I'd heard it spoken of as such. People left Aro's territory alone, even if they didn't know why.

Aro was one of the town's most respected council people, but few knew the details about him. I walked right past the cactuses in front of his hut, daring them to take a swipe at me. Again, they did not. "Smart plants," I said as I walked around Aro's hut to the back where he stood waiting for me.

"You've scared them into submission."

"Good."

He motioned for me to sit on one of two woven mats. I sat on the left. "We have known each other for some time," he said. "Though I have known your child far better. She was the best student I ever had . . . even if it took me a long time to see her."

I grunted.

"But you," he said, pointing at me. "Your name means 'she who knows.' What is it that you know?"

"My mother and father chose it for me, so you probably should ask them," I said.

"I am asking them, through you." He laughed to himself. "Okay, o. Give me answers. Tell me your story. All of it."

"What story?"

"The one of you. Who are you, 'she who knows,' mother of 'who fears death'? I am listening. I like context given in its proper context. Give it to me. I only know you as a wild woman's mother. Give me the rest. It's quiet out here, so I won't have any trouble hearing that non-voice of yours."

I considered getting up and leaving. I now understood what my daughter hated so much about Aro. He knew what he had and he dangled it before you while being an asshole about it. But then I considered why I'd finally come to him. Also, the fact that he remembered. He'd loved my daughter, he'd been her teacher. She'd *become* because of him. And so I stayed and released some of my anger on him, grasping handfuls of sand as I spoke.

I told him my life.

——

My throat was dry. I had been speaking for hours, both of us facing the desert. The breeze had died down. The sand dune in front of us had probably shifted a little.

"Ahhh, I see now," Aro said, turning back to me, his interest finally piqued.

"I *know* you have questions," I said. "There is still a lot I need to explain about my story. I will, I will." I took a breath. I felt so tense speaking my thoughts now. To speak them would make them real and maybe bring me closer to seeing them through. Maybe. "But I want to free my *people*; this is *beyond* my father's revenge," I growled, clenching my fists. My father's sister, their parents and brothers, his sister's lover had been killed by his sister's lover's Nuru family. They'd even killed their own son. The Cleanser had taken his sister and brought her back different. The Cleanser's mystic influence was linked to what happened. But now that I understood what it was, I understood that it was at the center of so much more about the Osu-nu people as a whole.

Oh yes, I had something terrible to kill. Finally, I asked, "Will you train me, sorcerer?"

Aro smiled. "Oh, I most definitely will."

CHAPTER 2

Rainfest

Aro told me to return in a week. In the dead of night.

I walked home that day in a daze. I'd finally done it. If I were honest with myself, it had been something I'd wanted to do even before my daughter began to learn from him. From the moment that Fadil told me about Aro. Yes, I had buried the witching (*I* had named it, and it did not matter what Aro called it) deep within me, but it could never be fully buried. Never. I still dreamed about it, even in those days when I was in the desert with Onyesonwu when she was a small child. And after Fadil told me that Aro was a powerful sorcerer everyone feared, I sometimes daydreamed about going to Aro and telling him that I was secretly someone people would fear, too. Now I'd spoken my story and my intent, and Aro had been impressed and said "yes." *I'd* manifested it.

I walked amongst the people of Jwahir, smiling. People noticed and smiled back. I went to my cactus candy shop. I'd hired and personally trained two young women Gisma and Makka to run it. I greeted them and took over the front area for a few hours. Gisma and Makka stood behind me in awe as I sold all of our product for the week.

"It's like you've charmed them," Gisma said.

"I don't think I can ever be that good," Makka added. "What's gotten into you today, ma?"

I shrugged, starting to pack up. "Today is just a good day."

The next day was the Rain Fest, which was why I suspected Aro told me to return to him in a week. Rain Fest lasts four days and during those days, no one works. This was part of why so many were eager to buy the rest of my cactus candy. People liked to serve it at night gatherings. During the day, there were sprinklers made from capture stations set up all around the market. People would stand under umbrellas, watch acrobats flip about, and eat boiled yam and stew, curry soup, and drink palm wine. I went to the celebrations with the Ada and, for once, I joined in the dancing at sunset when they ran the sprinklers so strongly that they soaked everyone. Something about the anticipation of training with Aro freed me up.

I laughed, I joked, and oh I danced. My loose garments, soaked with sprinkler water and sweat, clung to my body. I danced, letting my body move and revel in its motion, feeling the joy and energy of being alive. I let people see me. I didn't think of the wicked General Daib who'd raped me or his twitchy eyes and his knife with the scarab beetles on it on that wicked day. I didn't see my cowardly first husband Idris looking at me as if I were a corpse when I returned home after the assault. I didn't think of my beloved husband Fadil sadly watching me from a place where I could no longer touch him.

I didn't think of any of these things. I only thought of and saw the three men dancing circles around me. I had not felt the touch of a man in five years and this night, in the sunset, as the sprinklers sprayed warm sweet water, in the darkness, I allowed myself to have sex with two men as the water splashed down on us. They must have been in their early twenties. They were young. But such things happen during Rain Fest after sunset, when the energy is right.

I ran into the Ada as I left the town square. I was soaking wet, my garments slightly ripped, the alcohol from the beer I'd been drinking still in my blood. "Will you walk with me halfway?" she asked. She too was soaking wet, her normally loose clothes clinging to her body like a second skin. I wondered what she'd been up to as well. I didn't ask.

"Come on then," I laughed.

We walked in silence for a while. The night was warm, so my wet clothes felt great. I thought of Aro agreeing to train me, and I laughed to myself.

"You seem different," the Ada said.

I laughed harder. "So do you."

"I always come to this part of Rainfest."

"You do?"

"It's my favorite time of the year," she knowingly said.

"You're a married woman," I said.

"So are you."

"I am widowed."

"You don't see yourself as still married to your Fadil?"

I hesitated and then smiled to myself. It was all right and not even the Ada and her fixation on the duties of marriage could ruin this night for me. "He is free now, Ada. What of your husband?" I looked at her with a big grin on my face. I never asked her much about Aro but once in a while I liked to jab at her. I have never seen a woman so secretive about her marriage. The two were rarely even seen together in public, and they didn't live together. "We've always had an arrangement."

I didn't press her on it, but Aro did not seem the type to allow his wife to enjoy other men. If he did not know of her activities, the less she and I spoke of it and the less I knew about it, the better. We parted ways and I was glad to be in my home, alone. I walked in and stood in the center of the living room. My eye fell on the portrait of Fadil's first wife Njeri. A tiny woman looking down at me from the height of her camel. Fadil had always loved her and he'd easily shifted that love to both me and my daughter. Onyesonwu often stood in front of this painting and stared at her, sometimes she even talked to her. I often felt Njeri's presence in the house. Hers was a strong and kind presence that gave me comfort.

"You can't judge me tonight," I said. "Tell Fadil that I am still alive, and today was special." I laughed. "I have begun."

I slept well that night. All alone in that big house without my child and husband. It was a new time. I was all right. I was ready.

CHAPTER 3

The Mystic Points

I was well rested. I'd eaten a light breakfast. My shop was under the care of Gisma and Makka. I took my time. The morning was warm and Jwahir was just waking up. Many greeted me as I passed them and I realized that, unlike before the change, I was now truly part of Jwahir. Accepted. I was no longer the woman with the wild, dangerous daughter. To everyone but Aro, Onyesonwu had never lived past infancy. As I walked the dusty path to Aro's hut, I began to weep.

"My daughter, Onyesonwu, my hope." My tears flowed freely as I slowly walked. I couldn't feel her as I used to. I wiped my tears when I reached his gate of cactuses. Aro was waiting there at his hut's entrance. I paused, looking at the last cactus. Then I stepped up to it and touched my index finger to one of its thorns.

I gasped when I felt the cactus shudder. But its thorn still did not pierce my flesh.

"You are arrogant," Aro said, but he laughed as he did.

I shrugged. "My mother always said that when you want someone to truly understand you, you look them in the eye. A cactus's eyes are their thorns." Those cactuses would never take a swipe at me as they did with my daughter. We went inside his hut where despite the heat of the day, it was cool. It almost felt like being underground. His hut was clean, not a speck of dust or sand anywhere. The floors were covered with green cloths, as were the walls. I wondered if the Ada had anything to do with this since her favorite color was green. In one corner was a large bed, in another were two wicker chairs and a low table covered with blue and green cloths. On the table was what looked like a silky white cloth with a map carefully stitched into it.

"Sit," he said, taking a seat in one of the chairs. I sat across from him and we stared at each other for well over a minute. I refused to look away, though I kept wanting to look at the map. Even up close like this, I couldn't tell how old Aro was. He could have been in his sixties or eighties. His face only told me he was "older." Like my daughter and I, he was tall, and he was strongly built, like someone who was used to maintaining every aspect of his home. His eyes were a rich brown and piercing.

He sat back, still looking at me. "You are terrifying," he simply said.

I frowned. "What do you mean?"

"Where is your fear? Where is your insecurity? Where is your doubt?"

I laughed. "Have you never taught an 'old woman' before?"

He pinched his beard and cocked his head. "I . . . I took too long with your daughter. I want to get it right with you. But if I'm to teach you, you have to be less terrifying."

Before I could ask again what he meant, he took my hands. "What do you know of the Mystic Points?"

"I . . . I only know that you taught them to my daughter and no one else. Not even her lover Mwita, who was also talented."

"Ah. I should have also taught them to your husband's first wife Njeri," he said with a sigh. "I'm not a perfect man. Women are more troublesome. A man prefers to teach a man."

"Yet Ani keeps sending you women."

"Yes," he said. "Unpredictable, bleeding, brash . . . women."

"Ani is waiting for you to learn," I snapped. "So teach me these Mystic Points. Tell me what they are, what they're used for, how they can help me, how I can practice them."

His hands shook. Only for a moment, but I saw. He truly did find me terrifying. I wanted to smile. *I am terrifying*, I thought. I loved the thought very much. Daib should have feared me. Fadil was courageous, so he was fine with a terrifying wife. My first husband Idris was just stupid, so he never thought to fear me.

Aro took my hands again and squeezed them. "Everything seeks balance. The truth is in the voice, the perspective, the existence of many. Therefore, the Golden Rule of the sorcerer is golden. Speak these words after me, Najeeba. And as you speak them, shut your eyes and imagine shining, solid, sunlike gold: 'The Golden Rule is to let the eagle and the hawk perch.'"

I shut my eyes and imagined the gold of sunset as I flew over the desert as the kponyungo. "The Golden Rule is to let the eagle and the hawk perch," I repeated.

"Let the camel and the fox drink."

"Let the camel and the fox drink."

He released my hands. "Open your eyes." I did. "The Golden Rule is the foundation of everything I'm about to teach you. Tolerant, welcoming, open space for everything." He paused and then stood up. He was restless, uncomfortable, but excited, too. "Let's go outside."

We walked far beyond his hut. His gait was swift and, despite my long legs, I had to work to keep up with him. There were clouds in the sky and I was glad because they covered the sun, making the heat more bearable.

"Do you like the desert?"

"I love it," I said.

"Like mother like daughter."

"She was born in it . . . and in many ways, so was I, multiple times."

"It is in you and that is good. You'll need to draw from it."

We walked for a while longer. "You were at the Rain Fest," he said.

I tensed up. "Yes."

He held a hand up. "Don't worry about my wife. There's nothing she can do without me knowing. You, on the other hand, are now my responsibility."

He glanced at me. "Those boys you had sex with were clearly too stupid to be terrified of you. You must enjoy that."

I narrowed my eyes at him. "I enjoy men, if that's what you are asking."

"Young ones."

"If I am attracted to them, yes."

"Well, you are officially in training now," he said. "This is why training women is an issue. You are in your forties, right?"

"Yes."

"You can still have children."

I stopped walking. I pressed my lips together. I shut my eyes and clenched my fist. Only once had I spoken to Fadil about having children and it was a very brief conversation that we never revisited.

Aro's voice was gentle. Gentler than I'd thought he was capable of. "You can, Najeeba," he said. "Now."

I gasped, feeling prickly all over my body. Shutting my eyes, I sobbed. Then I just crumbled to the ground. "Ooooh," I breathed. I'd dreamed of having three children with my first husband Idris. Daib had snatched that dream from me, and Ani had given me Onyesonwu. But after her, it was as if the cruel sorcerer had cauterized my womb. Fadil and I were together for ten years and I never conceived, despite the fact that we'd made love very often and I had regular and normal periods. Fadil had gone to the doctor and they'd used a piece of technology to check him, and he was fertile. I'd never gone to be checked. I didn't need to. I'd stopped wanting more children after Onyesonwu, anyway.

My emotion now was not because I wanted a baby. It was the *possibility*. To have the possibility now, because Onyesonwu had changed everything, meant that Daib's curse on my body was broken. On top of this, the existence of the possibility made me feel that much farther from Onyesonwu. She'd never existed in a time when I could have more children.

Aro sat down with me as I shed that very specific sorrow right there in the desert. When I stood up, I felt sad, but also oddly renewed.

"Najeeba, you must understand what could happen if you conceived while training," he slowly said.

"Huh?" I grunted, wiping my face with the heels of my hands.

"If a sorcerer-in-training conceives, your training may be disrupted. Your control may be unpredictable and your power, your strength may be too much. You'd risk a lot more than your own and your child's life." He paused, looking Najeeba hard in the eye. "It happened to a woman long ago. She was learning the Points. She probably had conceived a day before. It was too soon for her teacher to know it. When she tried a standard lesson, it could have been water gazing or even a meditation, her abilities flared wildly. Strong. Terrifying. She, her teacher, and the entire town were wiped out. They vanished, as if nothing was ever there but sand and scrub bushes. I told this to your daughter and I tell this to you: You are now on the road to something powerful but unstable. Do you understand?"

I listened to his story. I heard it well. I wondered how anyone could know that this happened if everyone was wiped out. But all I was focused on was the fact that I could now have children. It was possible. Ah, the knowledge of it, the feeling of that knowledge was like cool pure water when I am thirsty. I only had to drink it.

We started walking back to Aro's hut and, as we walked, he linked his arm with mine, holding me up, guiding me, as he recited, "The Mystic Points are aspects of everything. A sorcerer can manipulate them with his tools to make things happen. It's not the 'magic' of children's stories. It's not 'magic,' so never use that silly word for what I show you. To work the Points is far beyond any juju."

I listened, quiet and open to his words.

"Okike, Alusi, Mmuo, Uwa. Say them."

"Okike, Alusi, Mmuo, Uwa," I repeated.

"These are the names of the four Mystic Points."

"Okike sounds like Okeke. Are they related?"

"Your daughter asked the same question. It's just linguistic coincidence. No relation." He paused, frowning. "Are we even called 'Okeke' anymore? I have not considered this."

I nodded. The change Onyesonwu caused fixed the disease of the Great Book. Did that fix change even the names we called ourselves? Was there any "tribe" anymore? Somehow I suspected there was. "Well, we are all still brown people of the Old Africa," I said, patting my arms and face. "It is human to name difference."

"True," he said. "Ah, it is strange to navigate this change. It is like being two people, having two awarenesses. You don't just know of the two times on a theoretical level, you can *feel* them."

"It gives me a headache sometimes," I said.

"Let's call those times before your daughter healed everything the Before and let's call now the Now."

"The Before and the Now." I nodded. "Okay."

"The Mystic Points remain the same no matter the universe or time or space. Sola once told me this. So that is good."

"Who is Sola?"

"You will know soon enough," he said, waving a hand. Then he taught each of the Mystic Points to me. This was barely the beginning, but it already explained so much. The Mystic Points were very old. When he spoke of them, he spoke of them in the Before *and* the Now, and this made me understand them more.

The Uwa Point signifies the physical world. It includes the body. So this is where you deal with death, change, life, connection. The Mmuo Point is all about the "wilderness," the spiritual world, the mystical world. Aro did not say this, but the way that I understood it was that the Mmuo Point and the Uwa Point are lovers because physical and spiritual are attracted to one another, repelled by each other, have much in common, and are constantly exchanging.

The Alusi Point represents non-Uwa beings. This includes spirits, deities, and those forces that cannot be named or explained but just are. This made me think of the glowing pink salt cube my father found that day and those who came to claim it that night.

The Uwa world is overseen by Alusi in the wilderness, though many believe it is the other way around.

The fourth mystic Point, the Okike Point is the Creator. "This point cannot be touched," Aro said. "There is no tool that can turn the back of the Creator toward what It has created." By this time we were back at his hut. "We call the sorcerer's toolbox, that contains the sorcerer's tools, Bushcraft." He stopped talking and waited.

I leaned against the side of the hut, thinking, rolling it all over in my head, connecting it to all I had been through and all that I could do. I felt dizzy, the potential of all I was going to learn a sudden weight on me. Aro patted my shoulder, and I flinched.

"You will spend the night here," he said, stepping back. For a moment, I thought that he meant with him in his hut, but he started walking away from me. He was inside when he loudly said, "You will stay in Mwita's hut . . . since he doesn't need it anymore." I could hear him moving away as I stayed where I was.

"Do you know what happened to him?" I called after him.

He didn't answer. I was glad.

CHAPTER 4

Haunting

The first thing that I understood about my training was that simply learning can cause things to happen. Okike, Alusi, Mmuo, Uwa, I spoke the names of the Mystic Points over and over. They were like a mantra in my mind, a song, and it was so strong that I had to voice them. Not for the first time, I wished that I had a proper voice to hear words aloud as I heard them in my head. My voice was a whisper, but the words had a weight. It was enough.

As I repeated the names, I went over the concepts in my mind. Turning them this way and that. Running them through the Before and the Now. They made sense in both. They must have done so much in the Before. In small and big ways, some driven by kindness, but some also driven by cruelty. Aro said that the Mystic Points were created by the Okeke, but the people who created it were not the only ones to master it. Daib had known the Mystic Points. They were great tools for my daughter. They would be great tools for me.

However, that night, as I lay on a mat in Mwita's hut, surrounded by the raffia baskets Aro said Mwita enjoyed weaving, I started seeing around the edges of things. I'd gazed at my sandals beside the doorway and see that just around the sides of them was . . . more, something else. I'd look at a corner, and I was sure that if I looked closely enough, I could see that there was something just beyond where it came together. I wondered if maybe I could peel away the wall's wood and find somewhere else behind it. The entire hut felt like it was on the verge of being elsewhere. It was a place haunted by another place. Its presence was a warmth pressing on my reality. All unlocked by the knowledge Aro had shared with me in a series of words. Because knowledge is power and language is powerful.

Nevertheless, I was terrified. I pulled the thin cover over my head and squeezed my eyes shut. Even then I could feel my understanding of the Mystic Points sinking deeper into my consciousness like a hot grain of salt on a giant slab of butter. I knew what it was to learn something like this so, though fearful,

I didn't shy away from it. I stayed present. It was uncomfortable, lonely, scary, and exhausting. But the fact was, when I had gone to Aro and asked him to teach me, I *knew* what I was asking. I was not a child who wanted something great without fully understanding what it took to obtain it. I'd gone into this with my eyes wide open. So though I squeezed them shut now, I learned, truly learned, the foundation of the Mystic Points that night.

CHAPTER 5

Initiation

I returned to my shop in the market in the morning. Gisma and Makka had come in before sunrise to set things up. By the time I arrived, there was a long line waiting for me to open the shop. I'd cultivated blue cactus candy that had a bitter sweet aftertaste. Gisma, the excellent saleswoman she was, made sure word about it had been whispered all over Jwahir.

"I added a hint of strong menthol I derived from mint leaves to some of the boxes," Makka said. "People already find you mysterious. They will think it's juju when they taste it."

I laughed hard. "You're both master marketers."

Our first customer was a grinning man I'd never seen before. "Good day, Oga." My eye fell on his left ear. He wore a dangling earring with black and blue beads on it. I froze. This was the earring the Okeke were forced to wear in the Seven Rivers Kingdom. It was the mark of a slave in the Before. "Your . . . your earring," I said.

He leaned forward to hear me better, people often did. But the lighthearted grin remained. "I know the style is to wear two silver hoops, but I've always liked this one. It has a familiar feel."

"Oh," I said. "It . . . it looks nice."

He beamed. "I only arrived here a week ago and all I hear about is your cactus candy. I'd like two boxes."

I made sure I gave him ones from the batch with the hints of mint. When I handed them to him, I couldn't help smiling back. His smile was contagious, and he was attractive. He may have been a few years my junior, but he had old eyes, like someone who'd seen much yet still knew how to find humor in it. He also had a long black beard with hints of grey that he'd braided at the tip. This was a style I was seeing more and more since the change and I liked it. "Is it true you own the Ogundimu blacksmithing shop?" he asked.

I nodded. "It belonged to my husband."

He paused, my words registering with him. Gisma stepped up beside me to help the next customer in line. Those two girls were such a blessing, smart business workers to the bone. "When I first arrived, before I heard about your cactus candy, I heard about Ogundimu Blacksmithing, but mainly because I was asking around. I'm a glass maker and it's always good to know the other people in town who shape things with heat."

"Have you stopped by?"

"I have met Jee, yes," he said with a smirk.

We both looked at each other and then burst out laughing. Jee was very very good at his job. He ran the shop wonderfully, hiring two apprentices after Fadil passed. But he hated people, as a whole. Jee must not have been able to slink away.

"How long did you last?" I asked.

"Two minutes," the man said.

We laughed some more. "That's pretty good," I said.

"I know how to talk."

I nodded. "I'm Najeeba."

"Oh I know."

"And who are you?"

"Dedan," he said. "Dedan Maathai. My glass making shop will be down the road from Ogundimu Blacksmithing."

"You are a Glassmaker?"

"Since I was sixteen years old." He reached into his pocket, brought out a tiny object and handed it to me.

"What's this?" I asked, holding it up. I softly gasped, feeling a bit lightheaded. *Kponyungo!* I thought. But with a closer look, I realized it was just a yellow red lizard made of glass. It glinted in the sunshine. "Oh. Thank you. It's beautiful."

"I make little glass figures in my spare time. I like lizards," he said. "Nice meeting you." I watched him walk away and then I looked at the lizard. I liked it. Very much. I took over from Gisma and quickly got lost in the work of the shop.

The sale of the mystery batch disrupted the entire market for the next hour. We sold every raffia wrapped box. The bread seller whose shop was beside mine, the father of my daughter's friend Fanasi, gave me a bottle of palm wine as Gisma and Makka tidied up our empty shop. "You are amazing," he said, laughing.

I took the bottle and slapped and shook his hand. The smile I brought to my face was false, however. It would always be a bit false, no matter how much I had come to like and befriend this man over the years. The thought of his son and his son's wife Diti, one of my daughter's best friends, still angered me.

The two had abandoned Onyesonwu, Mwita, Luyu, and Binta in the desert. And now, those actions were left in the Before; they didn't even remember what they'd done . . . because it had never happened.

"Thank you," I said. I handed him a small raffia box. "For you, as usual."

He smiled, delighted. I always saved him a "single" box of whatever I made, as payment for all the disruption my shop caused his shop, though the increased traffic helped with the sale of his bread. He unwrapped it and brought out the cube of cactus candy. He took a slow bite. His eyebrows went up as he chewed. "Sorceress," he whispered. My belly leaped. Did he remember?! Then his face broke into a grin. "This is the most delicious thing I've ever tasted!"

No, he didn't remember the Before. He was just enjoying.

I left the shop to the girls in the late afternoon, the hottest part of the day. I went home and took a long shower, taking care to scrub every part of my body, even the bottom of my feet, with black soap. I dried off and rubbed myself with shea butter, including my long bushy hair. I braided it into five thick braids that I rubbed with more shea butter and tied it back. I put on loose red pants, a matching top, my oldest sandals and wrapped my shoulders and head with a red veil. I wore no jewelry except the bronze bracelet Fadil had given me as a birthday gift.

I glanced into Onyesonwu's room. Nothing about it had changed, all her things were there . . . except the basket she had kept on her dresser. It was gone. I paused at Njeri's portrait as I thought of Fadil. Then I left my house. Heat rose from the road. The dust coated my sandals and feet. I turned onto Aro's path, and this was when I began to feel fear. I slowed down.

He was not waiting there for me at his hut, and I grew more afraid. I don't know what I expected, but it was not to do this alone.

"Walk past my hut and find a pillar of dust, one of your 'witches,'" he'd said last night. "Then do what your spirit wills you."

I paused as I walked to the back of his hut. It was dark inside. Maybe Aro was in there, but more than likely, he was in the House of Osugbo. At this time of the day, the House was cool and I'd heard there was a meeting of elders. Still, I'd thought he'd at least be around to see me go. So much of what I did was alone, even while in training.

However, he'd set up a nice goat skin tent for me with a raffia mat inside on the green cloth of his hut.

I smiled and crawled inside it. There was a glass of mint and lemon-flavored water beside the black goat fur mat and, somehow, it was cool. I sat down and looked out at the desert as I drank the entire thing. "Ahhhhh," I sighed. Delicious and refreshing. Especially in the heat. I got comfortable and shut my eyes. Inhale, exhale. I rose up and left my body as the kponyungo. Up, I flew. Then, gently, I did a roll and flew in a circle high above Aro's hut. I flew East, the sun behind me.

There were towns and villages this way, though nothing like Jwahir. I had never been to any of them. And I wasn't looking to now. I was looking for something far more temporary. It didn't take long. A witch. A big one. Coiled and blasting its way past some sand dunes. It reached high into the sky, almost as high as I was flying. I flew down, landing a quarter of a mile away. I stood there as my spirit self now. I laughed and said, "Yes, I'm definitely in the right place." My periwinkle garments flew about me. The wind of this witch could touch me when I was like this. I could feel it disturbing the air around me even now.

Aro had said that I should do what I felt the urge to do when I saw it. And so I ran at it. I felt the urge every time I saw one, even from afar– a need to throw myself at it. I'd felt this ever since that first time when I was with my father so long ago. It's hard to explain. The feeling of running as my spirit self was exhilarating. The closer I got to the witch, the louder the wind grew, the more I could feel the whip of its sands, a whirling funnel of brown yellow.

My feet left the ground. It took me.

=====

I was falling in blackness.

I hit the ground, the wind knocked out of me. In my body. I lay there for a moment. Back at Aro's hut. The sky was dark now and full of stars. I sighed and sat up. It was too dark to see, but I could feel that the mat was gone. I was lying directly on the sand. I groaned, sitting up. I stood and dusted off my clothes. Silky. These weren't my red pants and top. These were my periwinkle garments. I was still my spirit self. I looked around, realizing that I was not at Aro's hut at all. I was in the middle of nowhere. Cracked hardpan all around me.

There was no moon in the sky, so it was nearly black. Something shrieked in the distance. I shivered. I knew that things lurked in the desert that could harm even your spirit. I never walked the desert at night, but as the kponyungo I felt more confident of my ability to fight if something came at me. Then I saw it in the distance. Something glowing.

"Okay," I said to myself. "You're going to make me feel afraid before I get to you." I shook my head. "You're all alike." I used my kponyungo glow as I walked the long mile to what I eventually understood was a glowing tent. I approached it, frowning. It looked as if there was a fire burning inside it, a big one, but I saw no smoke. There wasn't even an opening at the top for the smoke to escape. But I could smell it. A sweet campfire smell, with a hint of some kind of herb or scented oil. It was not unpleasant.

When I reached the tent, I saw that it was made of a thin stretched material that looked brown in my light. I paused. The closer I got to the tent, the more afraid I grew. Now I was absolutely shaking. Was this what my daughter had gone through? She never explained to me what happened when she went inside this same tent during her training, and I never pushed her to tell me. She was different afterward, though.

There was a depth to her. It's hard to describe. But a mother knows.

What was the worst that could happen? This thought didn't help me. It only made me think of those spirit creatures who came after my father, brothers, and me when we were in that cave on the salt roads. Those things that caused my father's eventual death. "I am here," I said. Though I didn't know where 'here' was. I opened the tent flap with a steady hand and stepped in. I made sure I still glowed with kponyungo light. First impressions are important.

Inside was many times bigger than it looked on the outside. However, the fire was as huge as I imagined it to be. I glanced up and saw the night sky. How? I kept stepping through doors and winding up somewhere else. A tall figure in a dark cloak stood in front of the fire. "I thought you were going to fly away," he said.

"So did I." I walked up to him.

He pushed his hood back. His garments were actually a rich velvety red. He had strange pale skin. It was not like the skin of people who were Noah . . . and it wasn't just his skin. He didn't look from these lands, not Okeke or Nuru. Ghostly. A ghost who was very pleased with himself. His pale head was bald and he wore silver rings on each finger. He put his hands behind his back as he looked me over.

"Najeeba." His lips were thin, wet and pink.

"Yes."

"Aro did not describe you well," he said. "You are tall like your daughter, but your eyes are haunted, where hers were wild. And I didn't think you'd be so dark."

I tried to stifle my laugh and failed.

"What is amusing?" he asked.

"You're so white. *Anyone* is dark compared to you."

"Only someone who has not traveled much would think that," he said, cocking his head.

My amusement curdled, the smile dropping from my face. "I am more well-traveled than you can imagine," I said.

"You can't even see your grandfather's feet." I was about to bite back at him with more words when he quickly said, "Come. Let's sit."

We walked around the fire, and I saw that there were two wicker chairs set in front of it. "You're not a young woman, so I assumed you'd prefer this set up."

I gnashed my teeth. "I'm fine with whatever you offer."

"Better," he said, sitting down. He motioned to the empty chair, and I sat. It creaked under my weight.

"Barely have a voice, yet so loud," he said.

"I have other ways of speaking," I said.

He nodded. "Who sent you?" he asked.

"The sorcerer Aro," I said.

"I know that part but who is it who sent you?"

I paused and then said, "My father."

He nodded. "Eh heh. Do you know why?"

"Yes."

"Why?"

"He wanted me to stop the hate."

"A mere girl. A woman," he said.

"Yes. A sorcerer."

"The hate has been stopped already. By your child. Not you."

"The Cleanser still walks," I said.

"What is it you want?"

"I want to kill the Cleanser."

He looked surprised, then his eyebrows quickly relaxed. "Ah, now I see. That *is* interesting." He pinched his chin. "You do know it comes to all the Adoro villages."

I nodded. "But it is one. If I kill it in Adoro 5, I kill it everywhere."

"Correct, correct." He cocked his head. "Aro says you've been going elu . . . no, 'witching.' Is that what you call it?"

"Yes."

"'Witching, then."

"Yes."

"And that is how you saw the Cleanser so clearly. Because you looked upon it with your kponyungo eyes."

"Yes."

"You have been witching since you were a child. How is that possible? Who taught you?"

"I taught myself."

Again, his strange pale eyes widened then returned to normal. "It's a rare thing for a mother to impress me more than a daughter." He reached behind his chair and brought out a small blue jar. He shook it and set it down on the ground between us. "The irony is not lost on me, sha," he said. He grabbed the jar and shook it again. "Do you know what happens when one goes through initiation?"

"Not really."

"You may die."

"I'm prepared for that."

"There may be pain."

"I'm prepared for that, too."

"That was Before. This is the Now."

"It is all the same to me. I carry it all, Sola."

He blinked, surprised and a little angry. "How do you know my name?"

"I listen." I'd heard Aro speak it. I hadn't known who he was talking about then, but I could put things together.

"Egotistical," he muttered, shaking the contents of the jar into his hand. They were tiny bones, maybe those of a lizard or small bird. He grasped them for a moment. "I'll enjoy your failure. You are annoying."

I looked him in the eye and made my kponyungo light flare as I replied, "I won't fail, Oga."

He threw the bones and they tumbled and tumbled. A few of them flew into the fire, where they came to rest. He got to his feet and I did too. Slowly, he walked up to the fire, looking down at the burning bones; he didn't give the other bones even a look. He stood there for a long time, his back to me. I stood behind him, beginning to wonder if my confidence had ruined everything. The way the man had talked at me made me so angry. I'd been through too much to have even a great sorcerer talk down to me. I didn't tolerate anyone talking down to me. But I wanted the training. Maybe I should have been more reserved.

"Oga Sola, whatever I must do, I w—"

"It's time for you to die," he said, his back still to me.

My confidence drained from me in that moment. He was like an adze from the old tales, a creature who could suck your blood in seconds. This man had drained my confidence just as instantly. I was mistaken. I should not have come here. I had to get away from this pale man. I became the kponyungo.

I tried to fly away.

I could not fly away.

I fell . . .

———

My head rested against a cool rough wall of stone. I could hear myself breathing heavily but I couldn't quite feel it. I tried to blink and shake my head. I couldn't. Something was strange. I couldn't frown. I began to feel frantic. I couldn't *move*. No, this wasn't me. I was just seeing through someone's *eyes*, feeling what they were feeling. This made me more frantic.

Where was *I*? Where was my own body? I couldn't speak! I was just a passenger.

And so all I could do was watch as the person looked down at her hands. Yes, it was a "her," and her hands were strong and brown like mine. And they were shaking. She coughed, picking something out of her left hand. Then she looked up at the star filled sky. Whatever concrete place she was in . . . *we* were in, had no roof. It looked like that roof had collapsed inward. There was the sound of things crunching and grinding beneath her feet as she turned, stumbling a bit. She didn't look down, so I couldn't see the debris she stood on, but the sound was enough.

And then she . . . *we* were looking into the face of something terrible. She must have stumbled back. Her eye never left it. My eye never left it. All we could do, as we sat down hard on the ground of that place, was stare up at it, into it. I will try to put words to it now. It was white and unfolding and unfolding, maybe cloth, maybe flesh, layers upon layer, unfolding. Enormous. Maybe the size of a house, but you knew its size didn't matter. It was bigger than anything you could perceive. It was not alive. It was outside of life. Beyond life? Aro might have called this thing a masquerade, but it seemed like something far more elemental.

Yet it had a face. After the unfolding, so many unfoldings, it showed its face and it leaned toward me. Wide fishlike lips, empty eyes one could fall into, even me, despite the fact that I had no body to fall with. She was screaming now. Screaming and screaming and screaming and it was pushing closer. She was writhing in the debris on the floor now, but still looking at the thing. I could feel her withering as the face pushed closer. She was slipping away. I could feel her heart slamming, then losing its beat. The face pushed closer, white, expressionless, its many folds flapping softly.

We were still screaming. Her voice was my voice, for I had no voice. Its face was so disturbing, it stayed with me long after everything went black. I didn't even know things had gone black, despite the fact that I suddenly saw nothing. I was screaming. This was how Aro found me. I was looking into his face, but all I could *see* was the terrible thing. Its face taking my life.

My vision finally began to clear and I was looking into Aro's concerned eyes. "What is it!" I hoarsely whispered. "What IS IT?!"

"Come back," he softly said. "Najeeba. Come back. You have returned. Return." He put a pipe to his lips, inhaled smoke, and then blew it in my face. "Return."

"What is it!" I asked again. I couldn't stop myself. Even as I looked in Aro's face, I still saw the thing. It was behind him. Staring.

"Return!" Aro said, more firmly. He blew more smoke in my face. I don't know how long he did this, but eventually, I was coughing so much that I couldn't speak any more. And when I stopped speaking and grew quiet, the apparition began to fade. I calmed. "You have returned," Aro said, smiling.

I stared at him.

"And you were *screaming*."

I blinked. I was! I brought my hands to my throat and then stared at Aro. Speechless. I noticed the irony of this and laughed. As I sat up, I saw that we were back at Aro's hut. I was back in my body. Oh, I was so glad to be me again.

"Can you stand?"

I could.

"Can you speak?" he asked.

I cleared my throat. Took a breath. I said, "Whether I can or can't, there is no turning back now." My words came out in their usual whisper. I felt disap-

pointment and it intensified when I saw the same dis-
appointment on Aro's face.

"No turning back," he said, patting my shoulder.

The Ada was in Mwita's hut when I returned to it.
I threw my arms around her, sobbing. She didn't say
much, but she'd brought me some pepper soup and
dates. She watched in silence as I slowly ate and then
she took the plates away. She didn't return and this
made me sad. I yearned for her company, anything to
keep my mind away from what I'd seen. Nevertheless, in my solitude, my belly full, I began to feel better. I had passed my initiation. The final part of it was
experiencing death. What that woman had done and
then encountered was a mystery I tried my best not to
obsess over. I focused on healing and moving forward.

CHAPTER 6

Glass

"It's so . . . bright in here," I said, trying to play it off. The shop was full of customers and amazing glass objects, from orbs to plates to paperweights, even tables and chairs. Thanks to the side effects of my sorcery training, it all sparkled with exaggerated intensity. In the front of the shop, strategically placed in a sunbeam, was a giant blue globe. Of all the objects in Dedan's shop, this one sparkled the most, and it looked like something large and monstrous was dancing inside it. I let out a breath and turned to leave, but came face to face with Dedan. He looked into my eyes in that way he had when I met him at my shop.

"Najeeba, hello again," he said. He was wearing a blue shirt with burns all over it and a black apron.

"Hello," I said. "I went for a walk, and I realized my legs brought me here."

"What do you think?"

"The place is beautiful," I said. I rubbed my temples as a woman pressed past me.

"I'm not always in here. I prefer to create in my studio next door. The manager I've hired and her assistants mostly handle all this."

I glanced at the blue orb again and flinched. "There is certainly a lot going on in here."

"Not more than in your shop," he smiled.

"Which is why I went for a walk." I smiled sheepishly.

"Well, I'm happy to walk with you," he said. "I was about to take a break, myself."

"Perfect," I said, then I turned and walked out, hoping he was behind me. I needed to get out of there. Outside, I paused, letting the sun shine on my face, pushing it all off me.

"You all right?" he asked.

Relief. He *was* right behind me. "I've just had . . . I have a lot going on," I blurted.

We started walking down the road. "Like what?"

I shrugged and looked away. We were passing the electronics shop. I stared at it, noticing how the computers it sold were all operating. Back in the Before, this was rarely the case. Most computers were either dead or glitchy in some way. "Tell me about yourself," I said. "That will help. All I know is that you are named Dedan, you recently arrived here, and you make beautiful sparkling objects."

A group of scooters passed and I couldn't help moving closer to Dedan. There seemed to be more people than ever driving scooters these days. The ones I remembered ran on fuel made from corn; the ones I'd recently seen looked just as ancient, but were solar-powered. He looked at me for a moment but instead of asking me why I was so close to him, he put an arm protectively around me. I relaxed and then nearly felt like crying. I missed Fadil. I was glad when Dedan started talking. This was something I would think many times in the future. Dedan loved to talk, and I loved to listen.

"Well, I'm from the Seven Rivers Kingdom. Durfa, in particular."

"What?" I asked, before I could stop myself. In the Before, Durfa was the biggest and most affluent Nuru city where Okeke people were used as slaves for everything from hard labor to domestic work to skilled trader. No freedom, no pay, no rights.

"Yes, I've come *that* far."

I looked at him. "Did you . . . like it . . . there?"

He laughed, but it was a nervous laugh. Something passed over his face that wasn't joy. "Well, I'm *here*, all the way in Jwahir," he said. "That should tell you something." When I didn't say anything, he kept talking, "You want to know my story?"

"Yes," I said. "But if you don't want to—"

"No, I'll tell you. I know a lot of people have come here trying to start new lives, for . . . whatever reason. Well, *I* don't have anything to hide." We were passing an empty lot of sand where some children were playing. Their carefree laughter contrasted with what he told me. "I grew up in the Seven Rivers Kingdom." It was strange because he said this as if he weren't sure. "I was an okay kid. I went to school, learned to read, write, how to think, how to use devices. I liked the reading, especially when we got to talk about what we read." Again, that pause. "I was apprenticed to a glassmaker when I was fifteen. I've always liked to work with my hands. I'm tall and strong. I like colors and light. Heat doesn't bother me much. I was perfect for the skill.

"I was good at it. And eventually, I took over my master's shop. I met a nice woman, we married and had two children. We were happy . . ." He was frowning now. We'd stopped walking, children laughing and playing on the sand dune, not far from us. One of the girls was showing the others how to do a dance as she played a tune on her portable. The ancient and sturdy coin-sized super computers were mostly unchanged from the Before. "We were happy, and then about three years ago, I woke up one morning and she was gone. She just left. Taken the children, all her things. I had no idea where she'd gone and no one would tell me. No one knew why."

"I'm sorry," I said.

He shook his head. "A lot of people in Seven Rivers were doing that."

"Doing what?"

"Leaving their lives. No one can explain it. A friend of mine did it to his wife. Made me promise not to say a thing. I didn't. This man loved his wife and their children. But it was like one day he just . . . well, he said, 'I just can't keep doing it.' To this day I don't know exactly what he meant. When it happened to me, I'd been in that house for months, waiting for them to come back or at least get word so I could go find them. Nothing. When people left, they never returned. I decided to leave. East seemed like the direction of cleansing. I don't know why. But once again, a lot of people felt this way. It was easy to find people to travel with. I wasn't sure how far I'd go. I travelled for two years. Until I got here, and it just felt right. So here I am."

We stood there watching the children dance, and then I said to him, "Thanks for telling me your story, Dedan."

He smiled. "You're welcome. Thanks for listening. Would you like to get some puff puff? I've got twenty more minutes and I'm a little hungry for something sweet."

"Only if we can find the saffron kind."

We ate saffron puff puff and then spent another hour just talking. He didn't ask me for my story and I was glad. He didn't even ask me why my voice was the way that it was. I didn't know what I'd tell him, if he did. He always had a good sense of things. I laugh now because how good could his senses have been if he fell in love with a sorcerer?

When I got home that day, I sat on my armchair and went over everything about him. He had certainly been a Seven Rivers slave in the Before. Even in the Now, he knew to run away from Nuru people, to run so far East that everyone was Okeke. Onyesonwu had changed things, yes, but trauma leaves residue, even when it is corrected by expertly wielding the

Great Mystic Points. Dedan could still remember it in his bones, in his spirit. He remembered it so deeply that he still wore that earring.

Yet there was something so carefree about him. Like he was now who he was supposed to have been. Glassmaking was his calling, whether it was in bad or better times. He had that and it brought him joy. For those three days before I was to start with Sola, we saw each other as much as we could. He came to my shop, I went to his, then in the evenings, he came to my home, for I was not ready to go to his.

I told him as much about myself as I could. I told him about Fadil and that the woman in the portrait was his first wife Njeri. I told him about Onyesonwu, but I only told him that she had gotten married and now lived with her husband Mwita far away. I hoped he wouldn't learn that this contradicted others believing my daughter had died as a baby. I'd deal with that if it ever came up. I also told him about my meditations and that I was training with Aro.

"Aro? The Osugbo Elder?" he asked.

It was the day before I'd go to Sola, and I felt I needed to prepare him for . . . weirdness. "Yes."

"You go into the House of Osugbo? That juju place?" He looked scared.

"He is teaching me to be a . . . healer." I lied.

Dedan wasn't convinced.

"I don't go into the House of Osugbo," I said.

He seemed to relax. "Okay."

"But I go to his hut."

"Oh Ani help us. This man will make all my glass break if he doesn't like me, o."

I chuckled.

"I thought you were a shop owner and you own the blacksmithing shop, too. Ogundimu does most of the metalwork in Jwahir. What do you need to be a healer for?"

"You know how you feel about glassmaking? That's how I feel about healing."

"But I never see you heal anyone."

"I am learning," I said. "And you don't only heal people. You heal plants, too." I motioned toward my garden.

"Ah, I see the connection to your business now."

I nodded, though this was total nonsense. "Part of my, uh, training is meditation. So . . . if you see me sitting very still for long periods of time, sometimes for hours, just leave me alone until I am done."

"Hours?" he asked.

I laughed. "Yes. Hours."

He took me to his favorite restaurant, which used too much palm oil in their stews and served whole roasted legs of goat, huge sweet cakes made from monkey bread fruit. Oh I loved this place. We'd both eaten goat legs, and I ended up taking part of the huge cake home with me. He'd walked with me that warm night, and I remember thinking about how different life was now. I was in my forties, but here I was walking home in the night with a man I'd recently met whom I found beautiful. Like some teenagers.

We talked a little more about our lives. Since he'd arrived a year ago, Dedan lived in a house not far from his shop, in a part of Jwahir that was more active and modern than mine. More families with small children lived there and there were actual networks of people linked through their portables. The people here were much younger. He was known and liked in the community and he had a small kiln at the back of his house where he occasionally created his own glass works that he didn't share with anyone. "One day, maybe," he said when I'd asked if I could see them.

He was content, though I think he was also a little restless. And he already knew a lot about me, considering the fact that we'd only recently met. He knew a lot of people and apparently, a lot of people talked about me. "In good ways," he said. "Interesting and good."

I briefly wondered what the Ada and Nana the Wise would think of him. Briefly. We reached my home. "Wow," he said. "This place is old and solid."

"A house constructed by a blacksmith," I said.

He nodded stroking his beard. "The windows are well-made."

"Come inside," I said, after a moment.

He stayed the night. We spent most of it talking. We ate the rest of the monkey bread cake, and I showed him my garden. We were looking at my cactuses when he slipped an arm around my waist and pulled me to him. We both smiled, looking into each other's faces. I touched his beard. That first kiss was soft and sweet. Then it grew electric. I felt only a brief moment of hesitation. This was Fadil's home, Onyesonwu's home, our home. But before, it was Fadil and Njeri's. Njeri's portrait remained on the wall. I honored her every day, pausing and greeting her each morning. I decided that as long as what was between me and Dedan was good, it was fine.

He pressed me to the doorway, and we became more urgent. I sighed, as he came to know me. Glass blowers have strong hands. From the doorway, to the couch, and finally to the bed. So much passion and so much joy. Rain Fest was its own thing. This was something else. Fate has been cruel to me and there are times when I think Fate decides to make up for this in small ways. Oh, Dedan. He is one of those things. And to Fate, I say thank you.

CHAPTER 7

Training with Aro

It was a rare cloudy day and Aro had me run his capture station to collect several bags of water. All over town, people were doing the same thing, and I didn't think the clouds would last much longer.

"We take this device for granted," he shouted as we both watched the white coil of condensation descend like a controlled and very small witch with a loud WHOOSH. The capture station filled yet another bag with the cold water.

"I don't," I said. "Without it, I'd have been long dead."

"We all would have been. Never forget that."

I nodded.

"Bring that smaller bag and follow me."

I hoisted the palm fiber bag of water over my shoulder. It was heavy, but I am a strong woman. I managed. Part of being apprenticed was doing labor like this. I'd cleaned out his goats' hovel, swept the floors of both his huts, and did his laundry. We stopped at his tall cactuses. I walked past them almost every day now and they left me alone, but I still avoided them. I looked up at the one closest to his hut. It was wider than me and well over fifteen feet tall. And it was covered with thick strong grey spikes. Aro gently touched one of the spikes and whispered something to it. He turned to me. "Today you will begin with the Alusi point," Aro said. "Recite."

"The Alusi Point is all about the wilderness," I said. "The spirit world, the mystical world. The place that is outside of place. The playground that mocks life and death."

He nodded. "Good. There are many who inhabit the wilderness. To move through the wilderness and meet those people is to converse with the Alusi Point. You are not ready for that, though I think you have travelled through the wilderness before. It is a different thing when you do it consciously. Now, we will see if anyone wants to come and meet you here."

I glanced nervously at the cactus. "Why . . . what do the cactuses have to do with this?"

He waved a dismissive hand at me. "Water this

one. Give it only a little. It is an offering, not nourishment."

I lifted the bag of water to open the nozzle.

"No no no," he snapped. "An *offering*. You have to use your *hands*." He kissed his teeth, irritated. I dumped the bag on the ground and used the nozzle. My hands cupped, I brought the water to the cactus and then slowly poured it at the base.

"Now, gently touch one of its thorns. All this is to show it respect. Mmuo are not moved by humbleness; they like respect, they like self-aware confidence, and they like one who has true skill. These cactuses are more than they seem, if you haven't come to understand this by now."

"I have," I said. This was why I avoided them. "Are they—"

"No, but they are like anthills to a sorceress. They are one of the paths."

"Did you plant them?"

Aro chuckled. "No."

"Who will come?"

"First you have to ask."

"For whom?"

"Whoever will come."

"How do you ask for someone to come when you don't know who will come?"

"That is part of the lesson."

I touched one of the thorns. It was sharp. Painful. When I brought my finger away, there was a droplet of blood. I looked at the thorn. It was red with my blood, too.

"Relax," Aro said. "Focus. You have been initiated, they have already been watching you and waiting for this."

I felt something around me. And I could feel some part of myself asking them to arrive. From the moment Aro had said that I needed to ask, I knew who I would ask. Even if I didn't know. It was an irritating feeling. Like trying to remember something right on the tip of your mind but being unable to grasp it. Someone was coming, and I'd requested them. Not some *one*, some three! Why would I call *three*?

The air was vibrating.

"*Chey!* My goodness," Aro said, stepping back. "Everything you do is big." He looked worried.

The proximity of the cactus, as the air began to vibrate, filled me with terror. Visions of being impaled by hundreds of cactus spikes filled my mind. It was a cooler day, but still hot and the air suddenly felt thick and heavy in the shade of the dwindling clouds. I stood my ground only because I couldn't bring myself to move away from the cactus, as Aro had. The cactus did a slow roll, as if something enormous had rammed into it, causing it to move into a different time. A slower heavier time. The roll of motion slowly moved up, its thorns flattened and then returned to their original shape.

There was a low hum. I felt the temperature and air pressure drop, my ears popping. The first one appeared right in front of me, behind the cactus. The size and height of it. It looked like a tree if a tree were made of dead dried brown leaves that were actually rubbery twitchy flesh. Terrifying. The second appeared behind me, and I only know this because Aro told me later. And the third was right beside me on my left. I heard their humming in my ears. It pressed, blocking my ears, touching my brain, then my mind, my spirit.

"**I can teach you**." The words were not words; they were vibration.

"Teach me then," I said.

I accepted all they had to teach me, though I would not be able to bring it forth until I was ready. They gave me gifts, more tools for my toolbox. They told me stories. Many. I could feel them in me. They put a universe in me. And we also talked. I told them about how I'd learned to cultivate cactus candy. I told them about Dedan. One of them said Dedan was a "bridge," though I didn't know what that meant. We talked about my daughter and my pain. And that was how I came back to myself. I was weeping. My face was sunburned, because I'd been standing there for over five hours, face to the sky.

The moment I began to move again, Aro was there, throwing water on me and wrapping me with a damp cloth. "Come," he said, and I leaned on him as we stumbled into the shade of his hut. I lay on his bed. My lips were cracked. "Water," I said.

He gave me water and I drank. He gave me shea butter for my skin. And then I slept. And then the next day, I did it again. The same three came for me. The next day, it was the same. And then the next day, the masquerades were different, but still there were three. For two weeks, we did this. I did not see Dedan because I stayed in Mwita's hut. My sunburned face was aggravated and painful. My skin became very dark from the sun. I lost weight. And worst of all, when I wasn't communicating with masquerades, I was haunted by their voices, their stories and the lessons they were packing into my brain.

When Aro finally sent me home after those two weeks, three more days passed before Dedan came by. I was glad. In those days, I was able to heal my skin and mind a bit. I was able to begin digesting it all. I was able to acclimate to the knowledge I now held. For some days, I could only drink water and eat a handful of peanuts. So I was able to eat, but I was still strange.

———

When training in sorcery, everything is connected. Everything is a balance. And everything builds. So from the moment I learned to communicate with masquerades, I continued to do it, though I feared encountering the white ever-unfolding one I'd seen during my initiation. If it could kill that woman, by basically frightening her to death, it would do the same to me. After a while, I began to encounter masquerades in other places. Sometimes it was at the iroko tree near the center of town, when there were people all around me. The first time this happened was a month after returning home. I'd spent some time at my cactus candy booth, checked on the black-smithing shop, and then stopped at Dedan's to see his new project. He said being around me inspired him to start it.

"They're beautiful," I said. He'd piled a huge heap of the dry blue flowers with the purple stalks in front of his shop. They smelled wonderful, too. People were coming by to look at the pile. Some of them would then enter his shop.

"I didn't think it would attract so many people," he said, stepping aside as a woman went inside.

"You work around so much beauty, all the time," I said, picking up one of the flowers. "It's normal for you; it's extraordinary for the rest of us."

He shrugged, picked up a flower and crumpled it in his hands, letting the pieces sift through his fingers. "All I see is material I'll use for the glass."

"You're going to burn all this?"

"Of course. Once it's burned, we mix the ash of glass flux with the sand we'll melt to make glass blocks. It makes the glass easier to melt and shape."

"Can I take some?"

"Of course," he said.

When I left him, I was passing the iroko tree on my way home. The sun was near setting; it was the time when people came out to do a little more shopping at the market and to socialize. So when I paused at the tree, I was thinking of stopping by Nana the Wise's home, since I had not seen much of her in the last month. Ever since the Change, I had not seen much of Nana the Wise or the Ada. They'd become different people, and we'd slowly been drifting apart ever since. Even after the Ada had healed me, she gradually stopped coming by to see me. Sometimes she was busy, other times, we just didn't have as much to talk about when I stopped by to see her.

I was thinking about all this and hesitating to turn in the direction of Nana the Wise's home when I felt the air pressure drop. There were people walking up and down the road and no one else seemed to feel it. I was carrying the bouquet of Dedan's glass flux flowers and, for some reason, my mind at first thought the drop was due to the flowers. Slowly, I turned around, to face the truth. I could sense it behind me already, and there it stood. Was it the one I'd encountered during my initiation? I was so afraid to find out. But it *was* the tree. It was reaching so high into the sky that I couldn't see the top of it. And the sky was clear!

"Are you all right?" An old man had walked up to me, and I hadn't even noticed. I was looking up with wide eyes, my mouth half open. I slowly turned to the old man.

"Uh . . ." I took in a ragged breath, closed my mouth, and tried and failed to smile at him. "Oh, I am fine. I was just remembering . . . something. A . . . a dream."

"Ah," he said, patting my shoulder again. "It has been happening to many people, these memories of things that have never been. Don't worry. None of it is real. Look around, this is a happy, kind, beautiful place."

I nodded. "Thank you, Oga."

He patted my arm and went on his way. I glanced around. A group of teens walked by laughing. A man on a scooter puttered by. Three women were slowly walking in the other direction, in deep quiet conversation. I turned back to the masquerade who was so tall that it reached into the growing night. The sun was nearly gone now, which made the creature even more menacing. Hundreds of feet of thick red cloth covered in what looked like shells. I had only seen seashells two other times in my life, the last time being many years ago. These ones now were white, smooth, each the size of my fingernails. Thousands of them, maybe millions. The masquerade shook, making a clicking wave of sound.

I jumped back. "Why in front of all these people?" I whispered.

"It is the way of a true sorcerer," it said in a growling voice.

I bit my lip and forced myself to move toward it. I
sat at its base, my back against it. The shells felt awful
against my back.

"The way of the sorcerer is whatever the sorcerer
requires," it continued. "Nothing is written. Your
daughter knew that; it is your turn to learn it. Come
all the way up and meet me."

"I'll be vulnerable."

"This is your home, don't you trust it?"

"No. I don't," I snapped. "There is no land that I
trust; even the place where I am happiest is untrust-
worthy."

"Everyone must eventually trust someone."

I frowned.

"You want to be a sorceress, yet you are so broken."

"Yes."

"You are still haunted."

"How can I not be?"

"These are different times. Your daughter made
sure of that."

"Different times, different problems."

"Come all the way up and meet me."

I walked away. I did not look back even as it laughed at me. "You cannot master sorcery until you let it go. Until you can no longer feel his flesh inside you!" it added.

I shuddered and kept walking, my legs shaky. Its laughter followed me all the way home. Then it faded away. I stopped walking and slowly turned around. I could still partially see the iroko tree in the distance. It was back to being a tree. In that lesson I learned that some masquerades would indeed do me harm.

———

Aro sat down beside me. "Today, you'll learn to bring something back to life."

"I don't like the sound of that," I said, frowning.

"Why?" he asked. We sat on mats behind his hut, as we often did. He stood, holding up a hand. "Forget I asked. I don't care. Neither should you. Let's go."

We walked around his hut toward the pen where the goats stayed. "Oh, no," I said, as he strode toward the goats. "My daughter told me about this lesson.

Why horrify the poor animals just so I can learn a lesson?!"

He groaned and turned to me. "It was supposed to be a surprise! How am I to pull your own ability forth when you are so focused? So aware of your own fear, your insecurities? Ugh, this is why old women make such poor students."

"Have I been so difficult up to now?" I snapped. "I've mastered everything *beyond* your expectations! I've healed quickly! Sometimes I've even healed myself! Have you *ever* had to repeat the Mystic Points to me?! I remembered them from the moment they left your lips!"

"You need to be humbler."

"Why? Aro, I know the facts! My weakness is my trauma, and can you blame me? I'm sometimes afraid. Sometimes I hate listening to you. I'm *not* a child. I know where I need work. But I also know where I shine."

He glared at me. He knew I was right. "None of that is the point," he said. "The lesson is to bring back life that has fled or been pushed out, it is an intuitive thing to learn first, not an intellectual one. The element of surprise is the path to learning this.

Something must *die* for you to bring it *back*. So now you know. How will you bring it back now that you know it has to die? You will be too busy watching it die; your panic will override your instinct, now. Your brain will jump before the skill that lies waiting beneath."

"How . . . how does one . . . ?"

"It is different for each sorcerer."

"What was it for my daughter?"

"Your child was Eshu, she could shapeshift, as I can. For her, it was through body and then listening. It will not be the same for you."

"No," I said, thinking it through. I looked up. "I'm a witch."

He nodded. "That is your name for yourself. I understand it."

I thought about the kponyungo. I had not known I would become one, I just did. But first I had to let go, only then could I receive the gift. I walked past Aro to his five goats. All five of them turned and stared at me with their strange intense eyes. One of them baaed at me and I smiled. It trotted up to me, and I touched his black head. One of his brown eyes had white fur around it. "No, none of them."

"Fine. I have a better idea. Come, we should hurry," Aro said. "But it's more difficult."

We walked through the city of tents, recent arrivals to Jwahir. Even after all my daughter had done, people, Okeke people were still arriving from the West. Most just said they were looking for a new home. Some came from the East now, too. In general, people were just moving around, searching, restless, curious, but they didn't know why.

"I came through here only yesterday. I do that sometimes, to welcome people. But also, just to see and get a feel for what is going on," he said as we walked past wide, often luxurious Bedouin style tents. Music played, women and some men cooked, in one tent, a woman taught a large group of children.

"What do you think?" I asked.

"I think that people are confused," he said. "A great wrong has been righted, but there are untethered ghosts still racing about haunting everyone."

"Will it right itself?"

"No. There's still work to do." He looked at me. "As you know." We came to a large corral of camels. Most of them sat peacefully, resting in the midday sun. My stomach fluttered. Was he going to kill a camel? That was even worse than a goat. I hadn't been thinking about how I would bring any creature back to life. Now the thought of having to do so with such a large magnificent creature was unsettling. Not that goats weren't magnificent, too, but camels were survivors . . . like me.

"A group arrived recently and they drove their camels very hard to make it here," he began. "They ran out of food and their capture station was faulty. They were too far from any other town or village. They had to push to make it. They have a camel that was dying from the strain. If it is still alive, this will be the one you will bring back."

"Ah, that's why you say it'll be harder. This is an animal who is ready to die, as opposed to one who isn't."

"Correct."

"I don't—"

"We can always go back to my hut and use one of my happy healthy goats who wants to come back to life, as I initially—"

"Ugh, fine. I will work with this dying camel."

He approached a lanky boy leaning against the gate of sticks. "Boho!"

When Boho saw Aro, he immediately straightened

up, "Oga Aro! Good afternoon!" He rushed over, looking nervous. "My Oga has gone to take his afternoon nap. I'm sorry. I can go and get him, but he is at his home. I'll run fast!"

"No, no, do not bother with that. Just show me to the camel that will soon rest long. Or has the beast died already?"

"Ah, MorningStar? She is still alive, but she may not be by the night."

"Yes, there is always one who is dying. Take us to her, then," Aro said.

The boy didn't give me so much as a glance, so eager to please Aro he was. He opened the gate of sticks and led us past several comfortable, well-fed camels. There were so many that it was like entering a different type of town, and it was nice. I made a note of this. I missed being around camels. They were surly, yet peaceful at the same time. They were familiar, too. When we came to MorningStar, I sighed. If a camel could be exhausted, this was the camel. She was too tired to sleep, too tired to move.

"Leave us," Aro said to Boho, who nodded and rushed off. He didn't need to be asked twice.

We were surrounded by unsaddled resting camels. Most of them had come a long way recently. The ones who were awake looked at Aro and me with vague interest. I could see the boy and the tents beyond, but we were mostly hidden. I stepped up to MorningStar, knelt down and patted the rough fur on her head.

"Is this better for you?" Aro asked, looking down at me.

"Yes," I said. "But I still—"

"Shut up," he snapped. "So you will bring this creature back to life, to the physical world. You will show it back to its body."

"How?"

"For me and your daughter, we work things through the body. You will work things through the spirit."

"What does that even mean?"

"That's for you to teach yourself," he said. Then he pulled a knife from his pocket and came at me with it! My first instinct was not to protect myself. It was to cover MorningStar with my body.

"No!" I said.

He moved around me and I felt MorningStar gently tense as Aro plunged the knife into her neck. Then she went limp. That quickly. Yes, she was truly ready to go.

"Bring her back!" Aro shouted.

I didn't know how or what. But . . . I let go and sat beside her. I came out of my flesh, hovering above my body, ablaze. The kponyungo.

"Ah," Aro said. "Witch!"

I looked around. Every single one of the camels was looking up, right at me. Me. Not Aro, who'd just killed one of their own. "Where?!" I shouted at them. "MorningStar!" I called in my kponyungo voice, frantically searching. What would she look like? Light? Mist? I don't know why, but I knew what I was looking for would be yellow. Whomever had named her MorningStar had truly known her. But she was nowhere in sight. I'd failed.

I heard a soft sigh, turned, and found myself face to face with a yellow glow. She was still lying on her body, a pool of blood gathering beneath her.

"You were not ready," I said to her.

Again, the soft sigh. Tired does not always mean ready to die. Sometimes, it just means tired. I knew this better than most. I'd thought I was ready to die after Daib assaulted me. I'd tried, first in the place where he'd left me and then again as I walked the desert. I'd thought I wanted to become a true Alusi, a spirit of the desert roaming and exploring forever. But I was really just tired. And my Onyesonwu gave me the energy I needed to recharge.

Where can I get it? I asked. And then the answer came. I pulled it from beneath my feet. Onyesonwu had told me about this after Fadil's death. She'd felt the energy from the Earth, that day at his ceremony, as she looked at the face of his corpse. When she'd wanted to bring him back so badly. I did it now, as spirit, as a kponyungo. I dug my claws into the Earth, reaching and pulling up something red that I could not see in focus. It was a blur. I fed it to MorningStar.

She sniffed it at first and then began to eat. I dug up more. And she ate. I did this until when I held it to her, she just sniffed at it and turned away. I returned it to the Earth. The other camels watched as MorningStar's yellow spirit stood up, over her body. I changed into my human form and then I did something that brought me back to my childhood.

I brought my hands back and then clapped them together as loudly as I could. POW! The sound was loud like lightning. When I was little, we used to do this to scare the camels back home. We loved annoying them because they were so dramatic in their annoyance. Now, MorningStar's essence shivered with aggravation, then her physical body was shivering. All the camels in the area stood up, groaning and moaning, their ears darting this way and that.

MorningStar was standing up, and shaking out her dusty body. I returned to my body, too, then slowly stood up, moving away. Aro caught me as I stumbled, suddenly dizzy and weak. "You've done it," he said, sounding pleased.

I couldn't respond. There was too much noise and I felt discombobulated. The camels moved away as Aro led us out of the corral. I looked back at Morning-Star. She seemed to be dancing, prancing around in circles and shaking out her fur. The blood on her neck was drying, but I could not see the cut Aro had made. "She's awake," I muttered.

Boho came running up to us, "What's going on?"

"Go and see," Aro said, moving quickly past him. "Your MorningStar has risen. Give our regards to her master."

We left him standing there staring at all the groaning camels, MorningStar at the center of it all, roaring and shaking her fur. People were rushing to see what was happening as we left as quickly as I could walk. When we got back, he led me to Mwita's hut and I lay on my mat. I must have fallen asleep because when I awoke, the Ada was placing a bowl of pepper soup and a large cup of ginger water on my table.

"I was about to wake you," she said. "I have to go. Will you eat?"

I nodded. "I will."

She left without saying more. The Ada and I were no longer friends, that was clear. The change had changed that. I missed her. I missed Nana the Wise. I ate the pepper soup. Its heat was glorious. I drank all the ginger water, and it revived me even more. But I was still weak. So I lay back down. Instead of sleeping, I left my body and went flying. And that was how I healed myself. I flew and I flew and sometimes I walked. As my human form and as the kponyungo. I'd return to my rested body. Wash, eat, talk to myself, walk, sleep, stretch. Then I'd leave again.

When I had helped and healed MorningStar, I had dialogued with death. If I had looked around, I wonder if there had been a masquerade overseeing me. Ready to also take me if I mis-stepped as a sorcerer. I had not considered any of this. There is a powerful part of sorcery that is the opposite of thought. And in those times, you flirt with your own oblivion. It's not even really your choice because you just do it.

You cannot dialogue with death like that for the

first time and not suffer consequences. I was already haunted, there was an open door that was always there beckoning me. If I had not come and gone as I did in those days, I would have died, be it by my own hand or merely because of actions I didn't take, like avoiding danger. Aro knew this, but he always knew it was my path to walk, so he left me in that hut to live or die, sending the Ada, who knew nothing of my condition and who was no longer my friend, to put food and drink in front of me.

Three days later, I stepped outside and walked to Aro's hut. "You're alive," he said, coming outside to meet me. I started weeping. Then he surprised me by hugging me tightly.

"All right?" Aro asked, still holding me.

"Am I?"

"Yes. You are doing well."

"It is scary."

"All roads to greatness are." He held me at arm's length. "You have gone the farthest any student of mine has ever gone. I fear that soon you will surpass me."

"Fear?"

He laughed. "You're reckless. But that can't be helped."

CHAPTER 8

The House of the Rising Sun

Dedan was building a glass house. This was the project he'd been preparing for that day when he'd gathered the large pile of glass flux flowers outside his shop. He was building the house one glass cube at a time, and I inspired him.

"Whatever it is you do," he'd said, "your mystery, it made me feel like looking at the mystery within myself."

Aro told me about the meeting Dedan had with the council elders to get permission for the project. "He is a strange man," Aro said. "I see why you like him. He does not know of the Before, but he is sensitive. I don't think this town has ever had any real artists, let alone one who feels his work is important enough to come to the House of Osugbo to request permission to use a plot of public land for a work of art. Most people would just take it." Aro said that what Dedan described to the council sounded like sorcery, and Dedan didn't realize it.

Dedan and I had only known each other a few weeks. However, this was all it took, according to Aro, for my sorcery energy to rub off on him.

"As I've said, you are reckless," Aro repeated.

I had never gone to see his glass house, but women in the market were always talking about going there. They said it was like a growing jewel. The day after I left Mwita's hut, after healing myself, I finally went to see it. If there was one thing I needed at that time, it was to see something beautiful. That morning, I showered, dressed in an airy blue dress, braided my wet hair in three thick braids, one down the middle of my head and two down the side. I coiled pieces of palm fibers on the ends, and they slapped the small of my back as I walked.

I strolled, my hands behind my back, enjoying the morning sun on my skin and greeting people along the way. Most were on their way to set up at the market. I'd been learning so much, healing, talking to spirits, minor shapeshifting, plant talk, meditation. I could feel myself becoming with each ordeal. I had felt what it was to die during my initiation. I had flown with Aro on several occasions, our favorite time was the same, the height of the day when the air was hottest. Aro was a vulture who loved the thermals, and I was a kponyungo who loved the shine of the sun.

I was different now from the woman my daughter had left to pursue her destiny. I was different from the wife Fadil had adored. "Will they even recognize me?" I wondered.

"They will," a female voice said.

I looked around for who'd said this, but there was no woman near me. There was no one near me. These days, when I asked a question, someone always answered.

Dedan's project was on a road a half-mile from the last Jwahir home on the west side. To the left and right, there was nothing but dry scrub bush and dusty barren land. Yet as I walked, I wasn't alone. More and more people were coming to gaze at Dedan's creation. It really was like a jewel. Today there were some men some yards away on a blanket sharing a pot of tea and quietly talking. Dedan said that a lot of men came here to have business meetings in sight of his glass house. I waved at them and they waved back.

I slowed my walk so I could take in the full

spectacle of Dedan's masterpiece. The hot breeze was blowing in my face and it added to my sense of awe.

"I come to look at it every day," a man said as he walked past me, heading the other way. "It's like a prayer."

I nodded at him, speechless. When had Dedan done all this? The glass house had no roof yet, but you could see what it was going to be. It sparkled in the sunshine like something from the night sky. Did he polish each block of glass every day? How did they stay so clear? Beside it was the kiln he used for smelting the mix of sand and glassflux ash. There was a huge mound of fresh sand beside the giant kiln. Dedan said restless children were responsible for collecting and cleaning it, picking out the twigs, debris and dirt. They also helped gather glassflux flowers for him when they weren't in school.

The assistants from his shop helped Dedan stack the glass blocks, but it was mainly Dedan working at sunset and through the night. He would be taking his break for the day now and I knew this. What he was building looked as if made of the purest salt from the same dead sea my brothers, father, and I used to mine when I was a child.

Most of the house was clear glass, but there were

intricate designs he'd embedded into it using various colors. All of the walls were at least five feet high, but the most finished wall was closer to eight. This one was striped with lines of blue that made a glorious design as the sun shined through it. The wall across from it had the same lines, but in red. And the third wall was yellow, purple and green, its design looking as if it would be a spiral. The floor was made of glass blocks. This was where Dedan stood, his back to me as he contemplated the blue lines.

"Now I see why everyone is always talking about this thing you are doing."

He turned to me and grinned. "Finally, you've come."

"It's amazing, Dedan."

"Let me show you around." He took my hand.

"This will be the front," he said, stepping to the part that had no wall. "I'm going to put a yellow circle at the top. At 10 AM during dry season, the sun will shine differently through here. The doorway will be made of a beaded curtain. I will use steel wiring and thread my own glass beads on it. You won't be able to enter without announcing yourself."

He took me to the side with the red lines. "The paths of before," he said.

I looked at him, stunned. "What?"

"These are how you see the world before the house enlightens you. And the other side, the blue lines, are the paths for after."

I blinked, trying to process his idea. He was touching on things again. His sensitivity was coming through in his art so strongly. He had no idea. "And this back wall, will be the fruit of it all," he said. "I don't know what it will look like yet. I will know it when the time comes."

I walked around it .

"You want to go inside?" he asked.

"Can I?"

"Only you," he said, nodding and taking my hand.

We went inside. As I walked, I looked down at the thick glass blocks that were the floor. *Salt*, I thought. *Imagine if this whole thing was that strange glowing pink cube of salt my father found. Would those horrific desert spirits come in the night to destroy Jwahir? What* were *those? Could they even die?* I'd never believed they were dead; they didn't even seem alive. I pushed these thoughts away. "Will the roof be glass, too?" I asked.

"Yes," he said.

"What about . . . will it survive the sun? And what if people . . ."

"Aro has said he will protect it. But only when I've proven myself by finishing it."

Now Aro was giving Dedan soft lessons in sorcery. What was happening here?

"You're going to be a legend," I said, smiling. "It will be like a second House of Osugbo. The first made of stone, the second made of glass."

He laughed. "Maybe Jee can make one of iron."

The idea of Jee spending time away from the blacksmithing shop to work on a passion project was ridiculous, however. "Jee only cares about money."

"I love putting my energy into this," he said. "It feels good to create more than practical things, though I like doing that, too."

We were standing in the sunshine that the glass had turned to blue, green, purple, and red. It was hot in there, and we'd both begun to sweat. He was wearing a thin white shirt and there were burn marks on it from his work. I leaned into him, he smelled like smoke and fire. I felt the kponyungo in me stir.

"Here," I whispered in his ear.

"You sure? There are men having a meeting just over there."

"They will not see."

"The house is glass."

"It's thick."

He was already lifting my dress. He pressed me to the glass, my bare belly against its warmth. I stared at a blue section of glass, the sun shining through it, and as he entered me, I flew upward, leaving my body. It was my first time doing this to him. The combination of the heat, the smell of the hot glass, his smoky scent, and the bright colorful light made me want to dance. I used to do this to my friend Obi at the end of our friendship when we were so young, when our friendship became nothing but profound sex. But it was never this poignant.

Maybe it was because I was older, maybe it was because I was now a sorcerer in training, maybe because I had been through so much. Or maybe it was just Dedan and me. I danced and burned and flew, and when I climaxed, I was pulled back into my body so aggressively that it was like I'd entered a tunnel flashing with lights and blackness. When I opened my eyes, we were on the floor, and Dedan was leaning beside me with a delirious grin plastered to his face. "What . . . was . . . that?" he blurted after a moment.

"Something I haven't felt in a long looooong time."

"I want to feel it again," he said. But then he held

his hands up as he tried and failed to push himself up. "But not today." He laughed. "Ani is great."

"Ani is great," I said.

Minutes later, as we stepped out, I didn't look toward the group of men having their meeting yards away. You couldn't see what we were doing in there because the glass was thick and it distorted things, but I'm sure one could imagine. I wondered if Dedan had cried out. I pushed away the thought, with a chuckle. I was doing far stranger things than being a sorcerer's student.

As we went back to town, I glanced back. Indeed, the men were watching us leave. "Do you worry?" I asked.

He shrugged. "Yes. But what can I do?"

CHAPTER 9

Sola

I entered Aro's hut and found him standing there glaring at me. I sat on one of his stools and waited as he continued staring me down, his eyes unwavering. He was wearing his usual dusty white kaftan and pants, he wore no shoes, the hut was smoky with incense, his big hands clenched and unclenched. And still he said nothing. I sighed.

"This is very annoying," I muttered.

After another five minutes, he put his hands behind his back and walked around me, still glaring. This time, he flared his nostrils and narrowed his eyes. He stopped when he was right in front of me and then he noisily kissed his teeth, dramatically drawing it out. "An old woman like you shouldn't be having that much sex," he said. "What do you need it for?"

I scoffed, getting to my feet. I understood now. "I am *human*," I said. "'Old women' are still human beings."

"You could have chosen a man who is benign."

"What do you mean?"

"He's no sorcerer, and he's not like Mwita, but . . ." He shook his head. "He is *not* benign." I shrugged and was about to speak, but then he added, "Don't bother. It is what it is. You are not pregnant."

"Is that what you were trying to figure out?"

"If you become pregnant during your training—"

"I know," I snapped. "I could wipe all of us, our ancestors and descendants from existence."

"Then stop being so reckless."

"I want to be reckless," I muttered. I was glad when he ignored this.

"Leave me. Sola will find you," Aro said. "Just go about your day until he does." He'd grunted to himself as he sat at his desk and began to scribble something in a tiny notebook. With each scratch of his pencil, a puff of sweet smelling smoke lifted from the page. He lit his pipe and blew smoke from it onto the notebook as if in response and then chuckled some more. I stood there a bit longer. I wanted to say more, but when he got like this, it was best to let him be. I left.

I went to my shop, where Gisma and Makka were preparing for the day. They seemed a bit annoyed to see me, which didn't bother me at all. I wasn't at the shop every day, and I was happy that I didn't need to be. I hadn't been there in over a week, spending almost all of my time with Aro or leaving my body at home and witching to distant places as a way to relax from the stress of training.

"Oh calm down, Makka," I said, tapping her shoulder. "I won't be here all day."

She adjusted the silent frown on her face into a sheepish grin. "Sorry, Najeeba. I get focused and like to do things my way. When you're here, you—"

"Get in the way, I know," I said. "Gisma can handle customers. How about you tell me what you want me to do?"

"Well," she said, "maybe stack the lower priced boxes to the side there?"

I nodded. Busywork was exactly what I craved, plus I didn't feel like talking to anyone. I was still hearing the songs of masquerades, especially when older people spoke to me.

I was finishing up the last stack when Sola walked into my shop. There were two women in there at the time, one was holding the hand of a young boy chewing on a piece of cactus candy Makka had given him. The child looked up and froze, his piece of candy half in his mouth. Sola wore the same thick robes, but his hood was down. The two women stopped and stared, too. Gisma looked to me for guidance, while Makka walked up to him. "Welcome, Oga, may I help you with anything?"

You couldn't *not* stare at his bald white head with his piercing eyes and rosy lips. I motioned for Gisma to stay calm, and I approached Sola and Makka.

"What is your favorite flavor?" he asked in his buttery voice.

"Well," Makka said, glancing at me. I motioned for her to go on. "All types are delicious, but me personally? I'm a traditional girl, and I like my cactus candy plain." She glanced at me again and I shrugged. The truth was the truth, even if it was our cheapest product.

"Give me three boxes of that, then."

As Makka took the boxes to the front to wrap up, I stepped up to him.

"Your shop is nice," he said.

"Thank you."

"You have a knack for this delicacy."

"I learned to grow it in the desert to keep my daughter happy."

"Yes . . . but what you have done here, with such a delicate plant, it could not have been done by just anyone, surely you must know that."

I glanced at my assistants, the two women and the child. They were all still staring at us. He stepped to Makka, ready to pay. While Makka handed him the boxes, I said to Gisma, "I'm done for the day." She nodded. "Help those two women," I said. Gisma was glad to have something to do, quickly rushing to distract the women.

"Many thanks," Sola said to Makka as he took the three boxes she'd wrapped up. He glanced at me as he headed out, and I followed. Once outside, there was more staring. I walked beside him, feeling eyes on me, judging, wondering, prying. I didn't worry about running into Dedan, though. This was peak glass shop hours.

"You don't mind this?" I asked after a while. We were heading toward my home and we had a long way to go.

"Mind what?"

I locked eyes with some women selling peanuts. "The staring."

"No. Do you?"

"Yes."

He raised a hand and flicked the nail of his index finger and thumb. Then he brought them to his lips and blew hard on them. The staring stopped. People simply went back to their lives. A few looked at us, but in a way that seemed normal. I relaxed.

"I'm surprised you care," he said. "You should expect and accept it. These are still the people who ran your child into the desert."

"Are they, though?" I asked.

"Yes. The song remains the same," he said. "Take me to your home, Najeeba."

Once there, he walked past me into the living room, his hands behind his back as he looked around. He ran a hand over the top of the old goatskin couch, paused at the metal table Fadil had taken so much care to forge and adorn with geometric shapes. He stopped at the edge, noticing the place where Fadil had signed it in his scrawling handwriting. "Warm," he said.

"It was our sanctuary."

"'Was'?"

"My husband and daughter are gone," I said.

"But you're not."

"I am not."

"So why is this place no longer your sanctuary? I can feel it, it's still . . . warm."

I only shook my head. It would never be the same. "The sky is my sanctuary."

He paused at Njeri's portrait. "Ah, this one. Your Fadil attracted sorcerers." He nodded and turned to me. "Let's begin." He sat in the very place in the middle of the living room. The very place I sat when I went witching. Adjusting his robes over his long legs, he said, "Come. Sit beside me. It's still day time, let's take a trip. Just the two of us."

I sat next to him and he closed his eyes. And as I watched, he went witching. I could *see* it happen. He was himself and then something about him . . . left. It wasn't physical, but I could still see it. I settled myself, taking a deep breath. After one more glance at the vacant Sola, I closed my eyes. I became the kponyungo and flew up through the ceiling, then the roof and into the sunshine of midday. When I saw Sola, I roared my kponyungo roar. Then I flew to him.

He was green and black and magnificent and three times bigger than me. He was a great lizard, but he was not made of fire and wind, he was not a spirit of the desert.

"Najeeba, kponyungo," he crooned. His voice was smooth and much deeper and more sonorous than his human voice. We spiraled up high, my house directly below. "Do you understand what I am?"

"I do, but I don't know the name."

"Which is why you need training. One must know how to do, as you do, but it is also important to know *names* when there are names. Understand?"

"Why are names important?" I asked. He suddenly shot east and I followed.

"Sometimes, names have a way of bringing things into being. Sometimes, names can bring things into focus. They can bring power to the named, namer and the name. It all depends. Would you have known how to become the kponyungo if you did not know stories of them from your childhood?"

I flew up beside him. "I don't know . . . I may have been scared for a while, not knowing what I was."

"Yes, you see now, the power of names. The name of what I am is 'dragon,' an old word and creature from a distant sad place I am familiar with, from my own childhood."

"Dragon," I said. As I spoke the name and looked

at Sola in this form, I knew I would not forget it. I also knew I could find Sola anywhere, if I needed him. "Can you be seen? And what do people see if they can?"

"They see me as I am," he said. "Just as they see you as flames. Najeeba, you know the stories of kponyungo. Don't you ever wonder about the real creatures? Or are you content simply appropriating their form?"

I felt insulted. "I'm not—"

"Stem your defensiveness," Sola snapped. "I don't have time for it. Folktales, woman. You know nothing about the actual creature."

"I was once given a book about them," I insisted.

"And who wrote that book?"

I did not know. I had never bothered to check. I'd thought nothing of the author. I had been a teenager; I didn't know better. But somehow this excuse wasn't enough. Sola was right. I was wrong. That book could have been full of lies for all I knew.

"Okay," I said.

Sola nodded. "Your arrogance is getting in the way."

I stayed quiet.

"You're a child compared to me and Aro. Old age, long living, much experience is a necessary ingredient to becoming a master. You're not even sixty yet.

What are you?" He spat fire. "You have gotten this far because of talent and fearlessness, and yes, some experience. You may have been raped and left for dead, but you were never timid, you never let anyone push you around, even as a child. This was how you were able to master your witching and then later, master your projecting enough to guide your daughter to change the world."

I had not told him my story, but clearly he knew every detail. Had Aro told him? I wasn't sure if I liked this possibility. And something else about Sola was making me angry. Maybe it was his tone of voice. I hated the way he was speaking to me. I flew faster. *Let's see if you can keep up*, I thought angrily. *Dragon*.

The land below was a blur now. I chuckled to myself, flying low enough to blow a wake of sand. I imagined leaving Sola in the dust. The thought was satisfying. I glanced to my left, there he was, his green body, trailing a wake of dust just like me. I flew even faster, trying to maneuver in front of him, so I could spray him with dust and sand. He was faster. Much *much* faster, and he did what I was trying to do. I was blinded, as I blazed brighter, trying to burn the sand and dust away before it reached my eyes.

"Childish," I heard him growl, his voice sounding

as if he were an inch away from me. I gasped, looking for him, and, in doing so, lost my concentration. I was flying low and I flew downward, clipping the ground. My speed and the heat sent me tumbling, I wasn't sure if I was tumbling in the air or on the ground. Touch was a different thing when I was the kponyungo, so it was a total loss of control. "For your arrogance, I'll let you learn this part on your own," I heard Sola say, more in my head than anywhere else. "Go for a walk."

I rolled and tumbled and then in a great spray of sand, dust, and hot wind, I came to a stop. Slowly, I uncoiled myself and found that I stood up, as my human form. My periwinkle garments fluttered as I looked around in the settling dust. All I could see was flat land with white and red crystals encrusting the network of cracks in the land. I was standing in another dried ocean. The salt had not been flash-dried into edifices like the place my father, brothers, and I visited when I was a child, but this place had definitely once been deep under water, and that water had dried somewhat quickly. Quickly enough to leave its salt on the surface. This saline sand began to burn beneath my ghostly feet after a minute.

I began to walk, my back to the sun. "I don't see the point of this," I muttered. But it was difficult to remain angry in the middle of nowhere when the source of my anger had left me. I sighed. He told me to walk, so I walked. There is something about being in places like this, all alone. You feel both enormous and miniscule. And for me, I also felt true, transparent. And my mind immediately went to my daughter and the clarity of remembering that she was gone.

I began to weep. Tears do not fall from my eyes when I am spirit, but the rest is the same. I wanted to stop and lie down. Why go any farther? I would wait for my body to die back at my home. Let me let go of this life where my daughter didn't even exist because she'd fixed its worst wrongs. Not for the first time I wondered if the fact that she was gone meant that she was also part of what was wrong. When she had done what she did, I couldn't even see the direction she'd gone, or if she'd simply vanished, or if she'd "unexisted."

On top of this, the vastness of the desert brought me back to my greatest trauma: When Daib ran me down, threw me to the sand, and assaulted my body. I moved through life with all of it kept in a strong box that I buried deep inside myself. It was the only way I could function. But while out here, that box came up like a huge air pocket in the ocean. I could not keep it

from springing open and letting out all of its nasti-
ness. So I had to feel it all.

Daib stabbed a knife into the sand beside my
head and a scarab beetle, a creature of life and death,
landed on the hilt. Even though I hadn't done so in a
long time, in that moment, I'd wanted to leave, to go
witching! Yes, it crossed my mind. Of course, it did.
But to leave my body in that moment, abandon it as
he assaulted it, to do this would have been an unfor-
givable betrayal of myself, an abomination. So I
made myself as small as possible in my mind. Daib
sang in a beautiful voice as he tried to destroy the
future.

The solitude of the desert, when I was far from
other humans, alone, in my human form as spirit,
brought me back to those hours and the hours afterward. And so, as I walked, I wept and wept. For myself, for Onyesonwu, for the person I would have
been if I had not been raped, and for the world that
would have kept happening if the rape hadn't happened.

"Oooh," I moaned, trying to shake it off. In many
ways, my emotions and evolving thoughts were like
sweating when my world got too hot.

I was so wrapped up in myself that I didn't notice

at first. It may have started as soon as I landed in the middle of that dried ocean. Then I realized the air around me was hazy. There was a hot wind, so I assumed this was the reason. Then the haze began to circulate around me. Slowly, at first. My garments could blow about, but not from a physical wind, it was mystical wind that affected it.

As a learning sorcerer, I had come to understand that in moments like this, it was best to wait. I stopped walking. Immediately, the haze began to whirl faster, more aggressively. It circulated but also started whooshing from beneath me, too, sending my garments into my face, as well as wrapping them around me. I fought to keep them away from my eyes. It grew harder, blowing up sand and dust. Was a witch forming? I began to panic. That had never happened. However, I stayed where I was.

I heard the flames before I saw them. Crackling and softly roaring. There was searing heat but in my state, it felt like a warm wind. The flames were at my feet, and then they spread all around. They burned the salt and the sand, filling the air with black and white smoke. I saw the first one high above, larger than Sola's dragon. Lean and strong like a snake, shades of fire, coiled horns, magnificent jaw. This was

a kponyungo, a firespitter. I should have been terrified because this was the real *real* thing. But I smiled
because it looked just as I did when I changed. I had
not been appropriating its image, I truly had been becoming one. Sola had lied to me . . . or at least he had
played off my insecurities.

In my vulnerability, seven kponyungo circling
around me, whipping up sand and dust and spirit
wind, was exactly what I needed. Then one of them
flew at and passed right through me. I felt its burn! In
my head, my chest, abdomen, arms, legs. I groaned,
falling to my knees. My legs got tangled in my garments, and I fell back down each time I tried to get
up. After a while, I lay there on my side.

They circled, low and threatening now. I held up
a hand for mercy. "Please," I shouted. Then I came to
my senses and became the kponyungo. I coiled around
myself, so much smaller than those who circled me,
but I blazed as brightly as I could. It was broad day-
light, so I was competing and losing to the sun. My
terror became my rage as I fed off the pain I had been
feeling moments before.

"I will not flee from you," I roared in my kponyungo
voice.

They flew lower, circling me more tightly. I braced

myself for one to smash into and through me. But none of them did. They just kept circling. Then they slowed and the dust and sand settled. Finally, they stopped, hovering there, watching me—massive creatures of flame, heat, and smoke. Each of their eyes like specific suns. I could not tell which one spoke to me, but its voice was sooty, deep, sonorous, and vaguely female. "What do you want?"

I paused at the question and then said the first thing on my mind: "Aren't you supposed to be friendly?" In all the stories they rose from the sands to befriend human beings in their times of need, even if it was just because the human needed someone to talk to.

"Silly stories told by human beings," it said.

Another spoke up. Its voice was almost childlike in its pitch, "You don't look like a human being to any of us."

"Then what am I?" I asked.

"What do you want?" the first one asked again. If I went by the smoke, the one who spoke was the one to my left.

I turned to it, "I don't know . . . I was sent out here . . . to . . ."

"What do you want?" it asked again.

The others began to produce so much smoke that it blocked out the sun. I blazed as brightly as I could to counteract the darkness. They responded by blazing even more brightly than me. I brought my light down; I could never compete with them. All around me was dark brown with smoke. I could smell it, though I did not breathe it. How can I describe being able to smell thick smoke without taking it into physical lungs? Heavy, cloying, but because I was in my kponyungo form, it was pleasing. "Okay," I said. I was an apprentice sorcerer. I knew things now. I was here. As I was. I was kponyungo and had been one since I was a child, and now I was a mature woman. These were great creatures, but so was I.

Slowly, I rose up, turned in a circle, meeting each of their eyes, willing myself to be strong and poised. I was strong. I was confident. I *belonged* here, even if my teacher had abandoned me. "Tell me about who you are," I said. My words made me feel bigger, despite my size compared to them. I blew out smoke and fire as I spoke. "I become you."

I paused, giving them time to object. ". . . but I don't know why. And I never asked permission. It is disrespectful. I would like your blessing."

"Who says you became us by *your* doing?" one of

them asked. I didn't see any smoke coming from those before me. I turned around and saw the largest one glowing in a great cloud of the blackest smoke. This one began to whirl and whirl, blowing all the smoke away. Within moments, the sun was shining on us all. It landed directly in front of me and said, "Are you so arrogant that you think you could become us just because? *We* did that. I did it."

I didn't know what to say. Then I realized I was standing there in my human spirit form now, my periwinkle garments fluttering about me. I stumbled back, shocked.

"Sit down," the big one said. I sat. The others flew away, some of them diving into the sand like lizards, some of them seemed to fly into the sun, others created a cloud of smoke and disappeared into it. As this smoke dissipated, the big one flew closer to me, wrapping its body around itself as it hovered ten feet above, its fires heating my face. "I blew smoke into you and made you kponyungo when you were fifteen years old, in that moment when your brother was watching you leave your body."

"Why?"

"Because I could. I do not need a reason."

I frowned and then asked. "What is kponyungo?"

"Kponyungo are spirits of these sands, this heat, this place that remains and will be. We have always been."

"Are you like Sola's dragon?"

"Ah, Sola, a human who impresses me. But we are not like his dragon. His dragon is from somewhere else and much younger."

"Why are you impressed with him?"

"He listens and he is familiar to us. If he is your teacher, then you must be extraordinary. He does not teach just anyone."

"Who has he taught before?" I asked. I did not come here to learn about Sola, but I was curious, and Sola did not answer questions unless he wanted to.

"He taught the man who raped you."

For a moment, I could not think. I stayed still as this information traveled into my mind and planted itself there like a seed. The big one waited. Was that a smile I saw on its great maw? It was. And it enjoyed my shock.

"You know me?" I said after a moment. "Who I am?"

"I have watched you for most of your life, in my own way."

"Then why didn't you help me?"

"Stay on course," it said. "Ask me about Sola."

I paused again. Wanting to insist that it answer my question.

"He taught Daib?" I asked, instead. "Who else?"

"You ask the wrong questions."

I understood. "Who taught Sola?"

"I taught Sola, for a time."

I frowned, trying to make sense of this information. But I couldn't. Then the big one reached down with one of its great claws and touched my chin. "The Mmuo Point focuses on the wilderness, a space that is beyond space, time, gravity, outside of life and death. I am the one who taught Sola about this."

"You are a sorcerer?"

"I am. Did you think sorcerers could only be human?"

I did.

"The Mystic Points are an Okeke art, it is their language for that which they could never control or understand. But the Okeke gathered that information from somewhere, and many practice the Mystic Points. For example, Daib is Nuru and he mastered the Mystic Points. Very clever."

I didn't want to ask, but I knew I had to ask now that I was here, even after all the strangeness my interactions with masquerades caused. I'd learned how to converse with masquerades in my own way, was I ready to do it with others? "Will you take me where I can learn?"

"That is why you are here. Come. Keep up. If you fall behind, I will leave you there to fend for yourself."

I barely had time to think about changing. It flew into the sand, and I followed. I had always flown upward; I'd never thought to fly downward. And when I did, a whole world opened up for me.

I cannot adequately describe the wilderness, the place where kponyungo go. It is not a place for words, though kponyungo are powerful storytellers. Though kponyungo sometimes delight in the presence of human beings. Often girls, usually women.

I can say that I was gone for a period of time that does not match up with our own. It felt to me like many years. I came to know that the one who made me kponyungo was named Sonnn and we became very close. I did not master all that it taught me, but the Mmuo Point, the point that focused so much on travel and spirit, is my strongest point as the Uwa Point was Onyesonwu's.

In that place, I faced and burned away much of my trauma. I remembered my power, how much I had before all the trauma and how much more I grew over the years. To be human is to be limited. This is not a judgment on humanity. It does not have to be this way, but we're not good at realizing the power we have within us. It took leaving everything behind for a time for me to truly understand. Sonnn grew me, and now I looked forward to returning to Aro. I wanted to show him how much more I'd become. I wanted to show Sola. But more than any of that, I was ready. A human can only be kponyungo for so long while neglecting her humanity.

───

I settled back into my body. The first sensation I felt was coolness, though the room was probably quite warm after such a hot day. I could tell it was nighttime. For a while, I did not move, still returning to my body. I opened my mouth and sighed, feeling the air in my lungs. Feeling the air move over my skin. Aware of my heart beating. I was still sitting with my legs crossed. I was going to be stiff. I flexed my hands and then my arms, my shoulders. I opened my eyes. The lights were on. And Dedan was sitting on the couch directly across from me.

I gasped. After all I had just been through, I could still be surprised.

He saw that I had returned, and he leaned forward, eyes wide. "What are you?" he asked.

It was a good question. I glanced to my right. Sola was gone. Probably long gone.

"That white man left a few hours ago," Dedan said. "He was the one who let me in when I knocked on your door. He patted me on the shoulder and told me, 'You can take it from here.' I was afraid to even speak to him. The man looks . . . strange. Who is that? I've been sitting here for hours, and you have not moved a muscle. How?"

I just stared at him.

"I swear, I saw . . ." He shook his head. "What are you?"

"I'm Najeeba, Dedan."

"Are you a witch?"

I laughed. He didn't.

"What do you want?" I asked him. My questioned echoed what the kponyungo had asked me so long ago.

"I want . . ." He leaned forward, an index finger in the air, a confused look on his face. He cocked his head and looked at me. "I want . . . to get to know you." He blinked, looking surprised by his own words.

"I like you. I find you interesting . . . and mysterious. But if I'm to know you, I need *truth*."

He had spoken few words, but there was so much behind them. I understood precisely what he was saying, even if he didn't. He sensed the Before. He wore the earring, and he didn't quite know why. His marriage had fallen apart, and he didn't quite know why. He had fled the West, and he didn't quite know why. What he knew was that there was a truth out there he couldn't reach. It left him feeling unstable, like there was an itch he wanted to scratch but the flesh he could feel didn't exist.

I gazed at his face for a long time. And he allowed it. I appreciated this because I needed to think. I needed to fully come back. It had been so long. His bushy brown-grey beard. His piercing dark brown eyes. His skin was a soft brown, despite all the time he spent in the sun, and it had red undertones that made me think of the mystical red people believed to live inside a giant sand storm. I looked at his hands, strong, rough, with surprisingly long delicate fingers. I didn't know enough about him, so I went with those first moments at the market when I'd first laid eyes on him. He was kind and he was curious and he was genuine.

I decided to take his life into my hands. My choice. So whatever happened afterward would be on me. "Okay," I said. I told him everything. I told him about the Before. I told him about my childhood and what I did and could do. I told him about my first husband Idris and how he'd been broken and then abandoned me. I told him about Daib and how he'd raped me. I told him about going into the desert to die. I told him about my wonderful mystical powerful world-changing child Onyesonwu. I told him about how terribly Jwahir had treated her. And I told him about becoming a sorceress and all it entailed. Everything. He listened. He let me talk. I brought him food and drink while I ate and drank nothing. Then I continued. The sun was up by the time I stopped talking.

Dedan was sitting on the floor, his back against my armchair, a steaming cup of honey sweetened tea in his hand. He took a long sip and then spoke the first words he'd spoken since I started talking: "So, you *are* a witch?"

We stared at each other. Then he smiled and took another sip of his tea.

"Do you still want to know me?" I asked.

He sipped more of his tea and said, "You're not a storyteller?"

"You know I'm not."

"I know." He put his tea down. "So everything you said is true?"

"Yes."

"Show me."

"What do you want to see?"

"Introduce me to a masquerade."

"You don't want that," I said.

"The kponyungo then. Become that."

"Are you sure?" I asked.

"The Before, that was . . . real?"

"What do you feel in your heart?" I asked.

He only shook his head, picking up his cup. "Oh Ani, what have you done to my head?"

I didn't show him the kponyungo. Instead I made him another meal. A breakfast of fried plantain, boiled eggs, and more tea. We ate and then without agreeing on it, we went to my bed, made love and slept until mid-afternoon. He left to see to his glass shop, and I spent the rest of the afternoon puttering about my house. I watered my garden. And as the sun set, I walked to Aro's hut. I thought about Dedan as I walked. He knew everything now, and the thought of this gave me peace. We had made love in the bed that

I had shared with Fadil, and it felt right. I smiled to myself.

When Aro opened the door, he took one look at me and said, "You risk us all with your reckless behavior."

CHAPTER 10

Another Lesson

Aro ran some water from the faucet and filled a blue stone bowl.

"Water gazing is an art, but it is also a sorcerer skill. You have traveled through time, so I think you will be good at this . . . which is why I did not just send you here alone; I know I need to guide you."

"Fair enough," I said. I was nervous. This was my first time setting foot in the House of Osugbo, and I kept wanting to look over my shoulder. I'd followed Aro closely as we'd entered the building, and there had been no one around, but it had *felt* like every part of the building was staring at me. It still did.

"This planet is mostly water, its consciousness is easily conducted through it. Where you sit matters. On the ground is a place of power, but there are places that are . . . naturally deeper. The House of Osugbo is built around an ancient tree."

"I have always wondered how old that tree is."

"No one knows, why don't you ask it?"

I frowned. The House of Osugbo was conscious and tricky. To ask the tree its age, seemed rude.

"Here," he said, shoving the blue bowl into my arms. Some of the water sloshed onto my chest. It was surprisingly warm. "It's like meditating. You still your mind and body, breathe deeply, but then forget about all of it. Then you lean forward and look. Do not let yourself leave. You stay. This is not travel. This is gazing."

"Be intentional about it," I said.

"Yes." He brought a thick yellow candle from the table on the other side of the room. He flicked his index finger and thumb nail, lighting it, something I'd seen him do many times.

I looked around the room. It was spotless and cool, a window on the far side that let in sunshine. "Does someone come in here and sweep up?" The floors in the House of Osugbo up to this point were dusty and sandy. This room's floor was shiny and even the corners were dirt free.

Aro shrugged. "The House takes care of itself. Sit there." He pointed to a slightly raised spot on the floor and set the candle down. Unlike the rest of the floor, this place was rough and grainy, clearly wooden. "That's one of the roots."

I sat down, crossing my long legs. I placed the bowl beside the candle and took a deep breath. Aro was looking down at me and it made me uncomfortable. What did he think would happen?

"I will sit at the table over there. If you need me, speak up."

I nodded, looking at the bowl I'd placed before me. I took several breaths and closed my eyes, working hard to push away the feeling that the entire building was scrutinizing me. I couldn't focus, however. Who could focus while feeling like that? Watched by not only Aro, but the House of Osugbo? Judged. Maybe even mocked a bit. Why did we have to come in here to do this lesson?

I shook my hands out and shimmied my shoulders. I blew out some air and then took a few more deep breaths. *Relax, relax, relax,* I thought. *What they see is what they see. Strong. Learn, Najeeba.* I focused on my breathing and my anxieties and worries gradually fell away or quieted. After several minutes, finally, there it was– the urge to become the kponyungo and go exploring. I smiled, relieved, yet stifling the urge. I would travel later.

I focused and hovered there in my body. I stayed like this for a while. Just being. An hour might have passed. I opened my eyes as I deliberately reached both forward and beneath. I let my mind wander to a different great tree. The water was calm in the bowl, the candle's flickering light reflecting on the water.

The iroko tree in the center of town was one of the first things in Jwahir that caught my attention. When we'd first arrived, I was focused on positioning myself in the market to sell my cactus candy, making sure that Onyesonwu was safe, and navigating the shock of being around people after six years alone in the desert with my daughter. Seeing and focusing on that iroko tree was my first time not thinking about any of that.

I had been walking past it on my way to the market one day when I noticed it because a strong breeze blew in that moment. I'd looked around and then looked up at it. The tree was majestic and towering, with dark green leaves and rough bark. I remember smiling up at it because in that moment, it felt like it took away all my worry with its magnificence. Its leaves whispering in the hot breeze was like music.

VIII   **AUTHOR'S NOTE**

it's her whole life. However, for the sake of understanding this She Who Knows novella, *One Way Witch*, which continues *after* Onyesonwu has done what she did, I'll try and throw the bones of *Who Fears Death* here:

For a short time, Najeeba had a good life with her first husband Idris. When they were both twenty years old, Nuru militants attacked their village, killing almost everyone. At the time, Najeeba was out in the desert with a group of women "holding conversation" with Ani. And out there, a special team of Nurus, led by the general and sorcerer Daib, came for them. When Najeeba saw the Nuru militants approaching, she'd looked beyond them, at her village in the distance. It was on fire. She screamed so loudly at the sight that the fullness of her voice left her and from that moment to the time we meet her here, that voice remains nothing but a whisper.

The group of Nuru militants raped every single one of these women.

Daib and his militants were bewitched with a juju Daib concocted that made them especially vicious. The juju also made Daib and his militants and the Okeke women they assaulted especially . . . fertile. Every woman from this group who lived became preg-

w. Wondering about
t had seen. There was
ject in the blue stone
size of a marble and it
hing drops about. The
er, and it was the wind
igh dried, fallen, oval-
bounced over a thick
ver it and then every-

oom. A grunt. The seed
d. There was white wet-
seed and the wetness
then it was tumbling
winds. For a long time.
in. And for a while, the
m came that turned the
itning. The noise was so
ters ripple. But no more
nd beneath its watch the
n the parching sand that
id debris.
e as the storm moved on.
clear that the stars shined,

the milky way glowed. Then BOOM! The crash of lightning seemed to come from nowhere, for no reason. And it hit the ground near the seed, burning the sand to sharp shards of black char and glass and breaking the seed open. The seed sprouted. More rains came. The seed grew and grew and grew. In the distance, there were other, older trees. One was squat and round. The House of Osugbo?

The iroko tree grew and grew. Its presence brought beasts. A group of wild camels rested in its shade. Others, too—foxes, snakes, tarantulas, desert cats, beetles, bats, and an owl in its branches. The tree was rarely alone. And then an enormous woman wearing green and draped in what looked like crystals and silver was led to lean against it, while a worried looking man, also wearing green stood over her. There were others, too. And soon there were tents, then houses, markets, more people.

Jwahir had grown around the House of Osugbo. But this iroko tree had been a place where people and other beasts had been stopping to have important moments. I was watching time pass in rushes and stops, so there is no way I could name every instance that I saw. But there were a few that I caught. There were many moments where people proposed mar-

Note

next part of the journey, 's daughter Onyesonwu's ale. However, Najeeba is up. Najeeba doesn't look ll forward with her. The er voice, her mind, her rehash for context from

riter, cannot summarize —not well. It's a story that hy it's a novel. Just as Na- h this trilogy, Onyesonwu o *Fears Death*. Onyesonwu o has come to her prison cuted by stoning. It is an ptop, presented as a book. full, naked, and haunted;

riage here. A woman wept over the death of her sister here. Four small children fought each other here, pulling at each other's hair and throwing sand in each other's eyes. A man hid from his wife here.

The moment I remember most was what threw me out of the vision. A tiny sparrow zipped into the tree just as a thunderstorm was about to burst open. Up there in the iroko tree's leaves, the sparrow chirped a song of alarm. It hopped this way and that on a large branch. Then a feather fell from it, fluttering to the tree's base . . . and it sounded like something inside the tiny bird broke, cracked. Its wing? Its leg straightened and bubbled out, like a bladder filling with too much water. Its chest did the same, the feathers pushing outward then falling off. The bird was changing and growing. Then . . . then I was looking at my daughter Onyesonwu. Naked. Afraid. Powerful.

I was seeing the Before. I remembered this day.

I was looking at water. Then I was falling apart. No I was falling backward. My mouth was open wide, as I tried to inhale as deeply as I could. Aro was already catching me. "That wasn't the future," I breathed.

"What?" Aro asked. "I cannot . . ." He shook his head, catching himself. My voice was my voice. I could not speak up. "Say that again."

"I did not see the future," I said, squeezing my eyes shut. "I saw the past. From the Before timeline."

"That can happen," he said. I wondered if he recognized the double meaning of his words. "What did you see?"

"The iroko tree," I said. "It also remembers. I guess, that is why. I'd thought about the iroko tree. I wanted to know what it had seen. I should have asked what it would see."

"But that was not what you wanted."

"No," I said. "And I saw Onyesonwu. I saw her change. From a small bird to herself." I took a deep breath. I had never actually seen her shapeshift. "Does it hurt to shapeshift? It . . . it looked like it hurt." I squeezed down the emotion trying to bubble up inside me. I felt ill.

"No. It is a part of us. It is what we can do. Does burning as a kponyungo hurt?"

"No."

"Don't worry about your daughter," he said.

I shut my eyes, letting out a breath. Calming. I opened my eyes and nodded. "Yes, I have to let her go," I whispered. *But how can a mother not worry about her child?*

"Clean up that water. We are done for the day."

"Wait? What?"

Aro only laughed and motioned for me to get the rag draped over the faucet.

———

The next time I came into this room to water gaze, I was alone. Aro said it was the first time that was dangerous for someone with my abilities. Because I was a traveler, my water gazing was volatile. If I got too ambitious and tried to see the end of the world or something extreme like that, I could have started something. I was not "experienced enough to finish what I started," as Aro put it.

"Don't bite off more than you can chew," he warned. "Now that you see how powerful it is, just practice softly. Play. Be your own teacher."

I was gathering my skills. I practiced with care. I played. I honed. Each lesson I was taught, I added to my toolbox. So it was not one thing at a time. It was all things at the same time, and then I'd add another thing and then that would become part of the "all things."

I was alone the second time I water gazed. I was in a good mood that day. I'd first gone in the early morning to the desert where I flew as the kponyungo for an hour. There was a wedding in Banza, and I gave them something to talk about by flying over it and making them think that Ani was blessing the union. Then I showered and went to my shop to oversee things until the late afternoon. Afterward, I went to Aro's hut to wash his clothes, and after I had spread them on the line to dry in the breeze, I communed with a tiny masquerade amongst his cactuses. It taught me to draw a symbol in the sand that it called goniya, a symbol that it said I should master. The goniya meant, "heat" and it brought warmth to the hands of whomever drew it. It was a minor juju.

I went to the House of Osugbo just before sunset. To my relief, finding the room Aro had shown me was easy. I'd had a long day, but it was nagging at me . . . I wanted to gaze into the future, I wanted to succeed at it, acquire the skill for my sorcerer's toolbox, my bushcraft. I'd never lost sight of why I had wanted to do this in the first place—to kill the Cleanser. There were things I wanted to learn in the future, but I needed to know *how* to learn those things before I learned them. The House of Osugbo seemed to agree. The room I needed to find was immediately to the left of the entrance. The giant mask was right there to guide me. I grinned and went right in.

It was empty as before, and there was the blue bowl and candle. I filled it with water and set it on the rough spot, then I brought the candle. I smiled to myself; I had reason to use the new juju the masquerade had taught me. While with it, I had drawn the mystical symbol multiple times in the dirt. And then I'd drawn it on a small piece of cloth that I brought out now from my dress pocket.

"Okay," I said, as I rubbed my hands together and shook them out. I clapped them together, rubbed them again and blew on them. I glanced at the door. The last thing I needed was for someone to come in. I knew not to close the door; people in the house were like cats, to close the door would more likely attract someone to come in. Then, more than likely, they'd stay and wait to see me try this new juju. The elders and scholars in the House were all as entitled, curious, and judgmental as Aro, even though none were sorcerers except him. Everyone knew I was his apprentice. They kept their distance, yet they were *always* watching.

No one walked in. I looked at my cloth and then drew the symbol on the floor with my finger. The shape of it was a basic series of swoops, horizontal lines, and a vertical mark that was the shape of a flame. I slapped my hand on the spot where I'd drawn the symbol and snapped toward the candle. A coconut-sized burst of flame flew from my hand toward the candle. "Whoo!" I shouted, jumping up.

The candle was a little singed, but it was lit. I laughed and sat down. The room smelled of burned candle wax, but otherwise everything was fine. I put the cloth back into my pocket. I didn't think I'd need it again. The sight of that fireball had burned the juju into my mind. I chuckled at the pun of it and then began to breathe to calm myself. It took me about an hour to feel ready. I closed my eyes.

There were two cactus candy cactuses that I was cultivating in my garden. One that was supposed to taste extra sweet and another that had a unique fruity flavor that I really liked. I didn't have a name for it yet, but the combination of the two would be glorious, to me at least, maybe to others, too. I only had one of this particular cactus. I'd spliced them together, and I was afraid I'd killed the anomalous fruity one. I planned to look into the future and see. Simple, easy, sight. I sought to see the destiny of the two cactuses in my yard in a week.

In my yard. Right now. I could see them. There was no breeze, the sun was shining down directly on both the cactuses. They were similar in size, shape and both were healthy.

Weeks prior, I'd planted them beside one another so they could get to know each other first. Days ago, I'd gently sliced and joined them. The twine that I had used to hold them together was thin but strong.

With my mind, I pushed, moved it forward. Closer. The tissue I'd cut on each that moved nutrients and water began to knit. I could see it. I could hear it. The cactuses were tightly connected, they were stable, they were changing.

"It will work," I whispered. I saw it all in my garden, up close. Much else was certainly happening beyond it, but all I focused on, all I could see, were those two cactuses becoming one. It was a beautiful thing to witness in such isolation. They were their own world. I opened my eyes, taking the moment to note how I felt. I'd just glimpsed into the future. I could do it. What a powerful feeling. There was no consequence this time except for a mild bit of vertigo when I stood up, reorienting with the present.

After that, I worked future-glimpsing into my sorcerer's practice. It got easier, even as I looked around more. I wasn't too aggressive about it. I checked on the iroko tree next year, whether I would become friends again with Nana the Wise and the Ada in the next five months (I would not); I looked at Jwahir from above over the next thirty years. (It grew. A lot.) I didn't bother looking into the past anymore, though I knew I could. I came often to that room in the House of Osugbo, and each time the house made itself easy to find. The house seemed to like me coming there to glimpse the future.

My training was intense and I did it while running my business, quietly mourning my husband and daughter, getting used to the Now, and coming to know and love Dedan. Dare I say, in all my complexity, pain, sadness, and growth, I was happy. For the first time in a long time, I was happy. I had burns, bruises, haunted and invaded dreams and nightmares, body echoes like leaky breasts, throbs of terrible distant memories of a burning torn vagina and a deeply bruised neck, and I even had a constant ringing in my ears from various jujus, charms. Within my middle-aged self, I contained the decades I'd lived and learned with the kponyungo in the wilderness. I mastered core aspects of the Mystic Points.

For three years, I trained with Aro and occasionally Sola. The one thing I still couldn't bring myself to do was fully revisit my past. To dig into my father's tragedy, the very thing that drove him to ask the goddess Ani for one of his children to become a sorcerer—the brutal killing of his parents and siblings by the Nuru family of his sister's lover. I couldn't look closely at the memory of my strange mother who loved me with all her heart yet was always so glad when I was away. I did not once go to the House of Osugbo seeking books that might explain to me what the Cleanser was and how I could destroy it. Aro knew this but he did not push me, he did not pry, he left it alone.

There was a door in me that was still closed. And with all the other doors open, with hot dusty wind blowing through them, there was a pressure building up behind that closed door. Whether I knew it or not. Maybe a part of me did know. Maybe that part of me didn't know what to do about it because it didn't want to open that one door. Training had been a lot already. Or maybe a part of me also wanted to just destroy everything, including myself.

But I was also happy. Many things can be true at the same time, sha.

━━━━━

I took the blue bowl from the House of Osugbo. I don't know why, really. It was an impulse. I'd been flying as the kponyungo earlier that day, and I returned to my body to find a masquerade standing over me. It was all black and made of folds and folds of singed cloth. It smelled of burning cigarettes and the living room of my home was foggy with it. "Try as you might, you will never forget him. A woman carries the DNA of any man who kindles the life inside her." It spoke the words directly into my ear, and they went right to my brain and began to live in my mind. Poison. I will never know why. Aro says some masquerades just enjoy doing things like that.

I coughed out smoke and shook my head like trying to shake water from my ears. It was too late and the words the spirit had spoken were spirits in themselves. I'd choked and wept, rushing to the shower to try and wash the poison off. This seemed to help. But I still felt unsettled, and more than a little angry. I went to see Dedan at his glass house and standing in his nearly finished creation in the height of day cleared me up. The long deep kiss we shared behind his kiln and the promise of more to come when we were both free also helped.

Still, I found myself deciding to go practice my water gazing. But instead of filling the bowl as usual and lighting the candle, I emptied the water in the sink and decided to leave with the bowl. I'd taken two steps toward the door when a group of old scholars came into the room burning something that smelled awful. They glared at me, and it was clear they wanted me to get out. I was fine with this because I too wanted to get out. I left, the bowl under my arm.

The House of Osugbo did not like this, and it took me nearly an hour to find my way out. A large dog chased me down one of the hallways. I was shouted at by an old scholar who told me that the only sorcerer who belonged in the House of Osugbo was Aro. Nana the Wise saw me as she was coming down some stairs and without a word, she turned and went back up. That stung the most.

When I stepped outside, I laughed loudly in triumph, my face wet with sweat and drying tears. Two types of salt. I strode home, furious and rebellious and a little afraid of my own actions and the house's ire. I slammed the door shut behind me and locked it. If Dedan came by, he would have to come back later. I filled the bowl with water and plopped it on the floor in the middle of my living room, a splash of water drenching the carpet. I no longer needed the candle. I was sad and feeling destructive. And I didn't know it but the pressure at that closed door was at its worst. I was in intense pain, even as I was happy. It is possible.

I meant to look into the future. I'd stolen the blue bowl. I was going to future gaze for the first time outside the safety of the House of Osugbo. Aro would have been horrified. I felt so destructive. I think there were tears falling from my eyes as I closed them. My mind was empty, except for my emotions. In this moment, I had no focus. No purpose. Nothing I wanted to see. My logic was shut off. All I had was my rage, outrage, outage. As I began to see, maybe I burned, becoming the kponyungo without even realizing it.

Because I was flying.

———————

I had great beautiful wings that were flames.

I streaked across the sky and the strongest thought in my head was the loudest: that I would never leave Earth. And then something strange that had never happened, happened: I was the kponyungo, and I was flying next to *her*, a woman with wings. Was I now in a folktale? A story from the Great Book? But though there were so many people with mystical abilities in the Great Book, a man who could walk through walls, a man who could eat glass, many who could shape-shift, there was no winged woman in the Great Book.

This winged woman was angry, and I could see tears forming in her eyes. They'd flatten on her face and drop away. I could catch bits and pieces of her thoughts, but they came so swiftly and were so gar-bled, that I couldn't make anything of them. And she couldn't seem to see me. Everything melted with her as she flew, and then I was flying with her over a place that I had seen before. A world where the buildings were made of glass and metal and stretched high into the sky. This part of it was drowning, though I could see people in crafts built for the water, boats and rafts. So much water. No sand.

She was starting to burn brighter now. She was crying freely. This woman had given up hope. It dawned on me just as everything went away and we reappeared in a broken place where more of those tall edifices that reached so high would soon fall. There was something brittle and cold about these structures. They would not last. What should have outlived them had not lasted. In a cleared area, away from the buildings was the fallen carcass of a massive tree, its diameter reaching thirty feet wide.

I hovered above her as she stood tall at the tree's stump, looking around her. She wore no shoes. Her great wings were spread. She inhaled, and I could smell it too, the smell of flowers and smoke, but mostly flowers. A beautiful smell in an ugly place. She touched the stump. She put her chin to her chest. Maybe she closed her eyes. She touched her chest with her other hand. She shuddered. And then flames began to grow from her.

In those final moments, I wanted to shout for her to stop, but she would not have heard me. So instead, I just screamed and my scream was a roar. *This* was how it had happened? What was she? This was no story in the Great Book! The Great Book was a lie! What was Ani? I roared and roared, even as the heat and flame and destruction this woman had released consumed everything, everyone, including me.

I was still screaming as I returned to myself. In my voiceless voice. Guttural. Eyes wide. Still seeing the entire planet Earth burning. Burned by her. This was in the history of both the Now and the Before. My daughter had not been able to change *this*.

That woman! What. Was. She?! For a few more moments, I was connected to her. "They made me. In the dark. Science." Her voice was rushed, breathy, low. It sounded as if she were right in front of me. More understanding. It was as if someone had punched me. Oh yes, the Great Book was a lie! Ani had not turned her back. We had done this. The "Okeke" was everybody, all peoples from back then. The Great Book was a lie.

I was still silently screaming, and I screamed harder. My ears popped and I felt something give in my throat. I felt warmth in my throat. Blood. Then I was hearing my screams. My voice! I screamed louder and harder. I stood up and looked up at the ceiling as if I could look right through it and see the sky. My face was wet with tears as I released noise from my heart, my soul, my brain.

"LIES!!!" I screamed. "*WE* DID THIS!!"

When I came back to myself and looked down, I saw that the blue bowl was cracked in half. The carpet was not wet because all the water had dried up. The floor where I was sitting was hot to the touch. If I had been away longer, would I have set my home on fire? I stumbled, my face wet, eyes wide, the back of my white dress soaked with sweat.

I wore no shoes. Just like her. I walked right to Aro's House. He was just leaving. Wearing a blue ka-tan and pants and his better sandals.

"What is wrong with you?" he called, when he saw me coming up the path. I could see his body language change. Every sorcerer teaching an apprentice knew that they could be creating a monster. And so when they saw their apprentice behave strangely, their immediate instinct was to prepare for trouble. "Answer me, student," he insisted. Where he'd been walking casually, he now brought his hand out of his pockets.

"Lies!" I screamed. In my voice.

His eyes grew wide. "What has happened?" he asked. "How did you grow your voice back?"

He didn't say "get" it back. He said "grow."

"LIES! IT'S ALL LIES!" I screamed, tears flying, hands shaking.

I strode up to him. He stood his ground. His hands stayed at his side. I was his potentially out of control apprentice, but he decided to trust me. I loved him for that. "Oga Aro, teacher, please," I pled, sobbing. "*Everything* is a lie. Onyesonwu fixed it but did she know just how broken humanity is? Did she *knowwwww*?!" I fell to my knees, beside one of his cactuses as he looked down at me.

Slowly, I saw his knees bend. He came to my level, in the dirt. I reached for him and he took me in his arms. I buried my head in his chest where I cried and cried.

———

I told Aro about my vision. He listened, spat with anger, and then said, "This is new knowledge to me. I . . . I need to be alone." He'd rubbed my shoulder and then quickly walked away. I watched him walk into the desert. When he was about a quarter of a mile away, he changed into a vulture and flew off. The memory of what I'd seen washed over me yet again, and I started crying.

Aro didn't return for three days. I cried through all three, unable to push the sight of Earth's death from my mind. Humankind had been ambitious, they had created and created until they created a woman who could destroy everything. And then she did. She'd destroyed more than most of humanity, she destroyed the planet. *This* was why there was so much desert. This was why there were caves full of technology that desperate hopeless people needed to preserve as the world burned and then dried up. It was a forever horror. Though I knew there was hope. There were green and greening places and the rains were finally starting to come back, thanks to my daughter. But the Great Book had been a lie, a way to explain it all away at the expense of a group of people. Every so often, I would get a powerful flash of the winged woman. I'd feel the depth of her despair. She saw no other way. She was probably right, back then.

"A woman who flies should not be weighed down with such a burden," Aro said when he finally returned from wherever he'd flown.

I stopped water gazing after that.

CHAPTER 11

No

Dedan's glass house became the center of Jwahir, even though it was on the farthest outskirts of town. Teachers brought their students to go see it. Couples went to see it at sunrise, when it seemed to blaze. People even began to come to see it from as far as Banza. There was something about it that opened something in people. Many would come and stand inside it and just cry, some would get a dazed or awed look on their face, others would just walk around it, touching the glass. Dedan said that one man came to stare at the sun window at sunset every day.

Back when Dedan had finished, true to his word, Aro came one night and worked a protective charm on it. Only Dedan could make any changes to it. To try and harm the glass house would bring uncomfortable curses to one's life. As far as I know, no one had been stupid enough to test the charm. Aro made sure to spread the word about the charm.

I'd also put my finger prints on it, though unintentionally. I spent so much time there, especially during the night, when I was often out witching. I brought something with me, probably due to what my training brought out in me. Dedan said he knew when I'd been in there for a while. "It feels warm in there, more alive," he'd once said. "There's even a glow in the lower blocks. Like there's a fire lit near them and it's reflecting." After a while, the glow didn't go away.

Nevertheless, the enchantment that was in the glass house came from its creator, the artist, Dedan. Over three years, he'd mixed, smelted and molded the glass blocks. When he was building it, there were days when I'd come there to find him sleeping outside his kiln. He'd work all night and then just sleep there until the morning. "The sound of the foxes calling to each other sounds like people out there, celebrating something big," he said.

During the years he was building the glass house, Dedan spent most of his days at his shop, making plates, cups, bottles, furniture, small sculptures. He'd help clean up with his workers. Then he worked on the glass house until the sun set. He spent his week-ends and rest days working, building it, then perfecting it. On the rare days when it rained, he went back the next day to polish it. He didn't have to clean it after Aro put the protection charm on it, though.

And as he worked, he thought about, fretted, questioned, pondered. He told me about it sometimes. "Something is inside my head. I didn't know it until I met you. Until I started watching you, until you told me," he once said. And as he said it, he'd played with that earring he always wore, even to sleep. Dedan had been a slave in the Before. The hate was so strong that though it had never happened, it was still there. Dedan was not a sorcerer, but he was sensitive and he was a conduit. Aro saw it, as did others. Dedan's art attracted so many for a reason.

And he destroyed the glass house for all these reasons.

The Ada came to my shop that awful day, not long after my voice returned. It had been years since she had spoken to me and when she came in and looked into my face, she paused. Maybe the echo of a whole other lifetime where she and I were close friends flashed before her. She blinked and shook her head. "Najeeba," she blurted. "You've got to come with me!"

Before I could react, she grabbed my arm and pulled me away. Once in the dirt road, she turned to me. "Aro sent me. Your Dedan has lost his mind!"

"What do you mean?"

She was about to answer, but then she gasped. "Your voice! You can talk!"

I nodded.

"What . . . Did Aro . . ."

"No . . . it's a lot to explain . . . but Dedan, what about him?"

"His glass house!"

"Oh no!"

He'd been having nightmares the last few weeks. He'd been quieter since he'd finished the glass house. I'd expected him to be happy and free, instead he was broody and reserved. When he'd finished, there had been a celebration organized by the council of elders to honor him. He was brought before the hundred people who came to see the house and see its creator. As soon as he'd finished smiling and waving, he quickly slipped away, going home. When I'd gone to see him, he simply said he was tired and pulled me into bed.

Now, as I ran toward the glass house, I could hear

the crash of glass. He was on the other side of the house. "Dedan!" I screamed. "Stop! What are you doing!" There was a growing crowd of people standing there staring. No one was trying to stop him.

He stared hard at me. He still wasn't used to my voice. "N-Najeeba? That you?"

"Yes," I said. "Please stop."

"No! Stay back!" he shouted as I came around the side of the house. I saw why everyone was staying away. He was wielding the large bronze hammer he used to break and chip away parts of glass blocks he didn't want. He'd smashed half of the side of the house, already. With the thickness of the glass, I wondered if his ability to break it was enhanced by Aro's charm. He was the only one who could do harm to the glass house, so maybe this also meant he could destroy it with minimum effort. He swung the hammer and part of the wall caved in.

"Oh Dedan!" I shouted, grasping my head.

"It's all a lie!" he shouted. His words sent a chill across my spine. "We are all happy here, right? Jwahir is beautiful, we are well fed, we have celebrations, we have water, the children are learning, the sky is blue and sometimes it is grey with *rain*! But it's not right!"

He swung the hammer again and more glass went flying. "Who are we?" *Crash!* "Why are we?" He looked at me with wild eyes. I glanced behind me, there were at least twenty people gawking at us. They'd moved around so they could see, while keeping their distance. There was a child in the front. "Mama, why's he doing that?"

"He may have been drinking," his mother said.

"I think he's been smoking igbo," someone said.

"Dedan," I said, keeping my voice low as I took a step toward him. "We've talked about this."

"The Before?" he shouted. "The Before is NOW! I built this to make something beautiful. It's clear, transparent, it doesn't LIE! But it's not ENOUGH. NOTHING WILL EVER BE ENOUGH."

He was about to swing again. I dropped into it quickly and then sprang only part of myself forward.

"**Dedan, stop**," I said, stepping my voice forward as Aro had taught me. I had no problem stepping out of my body, but stepping only my voice took a lot more careful control that I did not have yet, especially since I'd only recently gotten my voice back. Dedan dropped the hammer and clapped his hand over his ears, exclaiming with pain, cursing.

"I'm sorry, I'm sorry," I said, rushing forward and

putting my hands on his shoulders. Behind us, the rest of the wall collapsed with a crash. Dedan and I stumbled away from it just as the entire roof collapsed. Dedan threw himself over me.

The crowd rushed back. A cloud of dust rose up and for a moment, it looked like a winged spirit reaching for the sky. Freed. Dedan got to his feet, grinning, and laughing. "See! Look at it! Freedom! We deserve freedom!" His left ear was bleeding, but he didn't notice.

I slowly got up. The glass house was now a ruin, two and a half of its walls still standing.

"I didn't think it would be so easy," Dedan whispered, stepping toward it.

"Dedan, it's still dangerous."

"It was always dangerous," he softly said, flicking aside a large hunk of glass. "This is not how normal glass behaves."

"Probably Aro's charm," I said, but I was no longer watching Dedan. I was looking toward the crowd. Where the crowd had been. Only one man stood there now, everyone else had moved way back or fled. I squinted in the dust. I frowned and walked toward the man. I paused and shuddered, a wave of nausea passing over me. I clenched my fists, so many things rushing through my mind. I had learned so much. I could ask masquerades and some of them would listen. I knew how to cause pain. I knew how to heal and oh, I knew how to harm. I wasn't that woman lying in the sand wanting but unable to leave her body, terrified of the knife beside my head with the scarab beetle on it. I was that woman *and* so much more now.

I was feet away from him. A tall man with a long black beard, a Nuru man. I looked him right in the eyes. I knew those eyes well. I would *never* forget those eyes. I rubbed my hands together, clapped them, rubbed them again, shook them out. He watched me do this and this made me even angrier. I drew the symbol in the air. I'd practiced it all those times in the House of Osugbo when I lit the candle to water gaze. It now came easily to me. Goniya. My hands were warm with the juju's heat. I focused it and my hands grew hot. If I had looked at them, I'd have seen that they were glowing red orange.

I snarled as I raised my hand to snap my fingers toward the man. Daib. The man who'd raped me. The biological father of Onyesonwu. Standing. Right. There. Here. In. My. Town. Now.

Something stopped my fingers from snapping. Slowly, I looked. Another hand was holding my hand, smoke rising from it. The smell of meat cooking. "We do *not* use our abilities for that," Aro said, his eyes watering as he withstood the pain.

CHAPTER 12

Daib

Aro had followed him from the moment he came within a mile of Jwahir. He'd known that Daib was alive and had long ago set up parameters around town. "I saw him there in Seven Rivers," Aro said. "When Onyesonwu did what she did. He was there hoping she wouldn't. Then he'd limped away." So Aro knew Daib was alive and that it was only a matter of time. And when he'd sensed him, he'd followed him from afar. Daib had come right for me when he walked into Jwahir. No camel. No companions.

Aro stood with me as I faced him. Daib wore dusty but clearly well-made garments. His skin was probably darkened by the sun, but to my eyes, he was still strange to me.

"So this is you," he said.

I flared my nostrils, still smelling Aro's burned hand. My eye twitched as I gazed into Daib's eyes. No words.

"Do you remember?" he asked.

I said nothing.

"I remember all of it," he said. He looked past me, at Dedan and what remained of the glass house. "Seems *he* remembers something, too. Though clearly not much. That is why he has become . . . violent." I shuddered, fresh rage flooding my blood. Onyesonwu had lived all her life with people thinking she would become violent because of what she was born of. Daib had the nerve to step closer to me, that confident look on his face, as if I could not take his life on the spot. "Your silence is—"

"If you remember, then why have you come here?" I growled.

"She has a voice," he said, a smile spreading over his face.

CRASH! Another wall of the glass house was falling. Yet I didn't take my eyes from Daib and he did not take his from mine. Dedan guffawed loudly, standing beside the house.

"You do not scare me," I said.

Aro put up an arm now and pushed me back. I

glared at him, but obeyed. He was my teacher. "What do you want, Daib?" Aro asked.

He leveled his eyes at Aro. I took another step back. "You were Onyesonwu's master," Daib said.

"What do you want?" Aro asked again.

"And you are *her* master, too?" Daib continued. "Daughter, then mother. What are you chasing?"

"What are *you* chasing?" Aro asked.

For the first time since I'd seen him, Daib lowered his eyes, the bravado slipping from his face. He held up a hand and, after a moment, a large scarab beetle flew to it. Aro suddenly grinned. "Oooh. Could it be?" he said. "Atonement."

Daib said nothing, but his lips twitched.

Aro looked at me. "Stand down. You'll want to deal with this well. A sorcerer's atonement must always be honored. It is a juju, one that must have been evoked by your daughter, whether she knew it or not."

I snarled. "She did *not*. She'd rather have killed this man."

"Sorcerer," Aro quickly said. "Will you come to my hut?"

Daib nodded.

I was horrified. "You are going to bring him to your home?"

"This is duty," Aro said. "This is code."

"Bushcraft," Daib added.

I only wanted to kill him.

CRASH! Another wall went down. More laughter from Dedan. This time I turned around. "Dedan, STOP IT!"

"No!"

Dedan took down the entire glass house as people watched, and I couldn't do anything about it. The crowd grew to over a hundred people. Many even applauded! By the end, Dedan was standing on top of a pile of glass. I stayed and watched because it was better than watching Aro walk away with Daib. "Come when you are ready," was all Aro had said to me.

Once they were gone, I found that watching Dedan destroy his art was oddly satisfying. I was there for the same reason other Jwahirians were there. The destruction of such beauty and joy felt like breaking through a shell that had grown too tight, no matter how beautiful it was. People would probably talk about this for years.

I followed Dedan when he finally decided he was done. Together, we walked down the road in silence. I glanced back and saw the people crowding around the remains of the glass house. A man picked up a shard and walked away with it. Others were doing the same.

Dedan was walking swiftly now. "Where are we going?" I asked.

"I don't know," he said. He laughed. "I feel better."

"Good."

"But I also feel hurt."

"I understand."

"You can never," he said. But he didn't say it like an accusation. "You remember. I don't. I *can't*." He nodded. "But I feel better now."

"It was all just sand, anyway," I said.

He laughed at this, taking my hand. He pulled me to him and kissed my forehead. "From sand we come from and to sand we'll return. Just not yet."

"No, my love, not yet."

Dedan went back to his shop. Yes, just like that, he went back to the work he loved. His shop was full of customers who'd heard about what he'd done. They came to his shop with pieces of the glass house wanting to buy objects that they could store the pieces in. He sold all his jars, plates, bottles, he even sold larger pieces of furniture to three people who wanted the pieces of glass welded to it. All this, he told me later.

After I left him, I went to Aro's hut. I walked slowly. Stopping every so often to consider a bird, a lizard, the iroko tree, some children playing, a woman sweeping her front porch, a spiral from a nearby capture station reaching into the sky. I took over an hour to get there. Then I stood outside for another half hour. They were in there. *He* was in there. I paced between the cactuses. I was tired. It had been a long day. I was hungry. And I was angry.

I had been Aro's apprentice for seven years. By this time, I knew how he taught and I knew what he expected. Aro was not going to come out. He was not going to make this easier on me. It didn't matter how much it hurt. I groaned, clenching my fists. The sun was starting to go down. Another half hour passed.

"Go," I whispered to myself. Then I said it louder. "Go." I went inside. No one was there. They were in the back. With Sola. Three men standing together. I froze. Daib had been taught by Sola, until he went wrong. Sola had never explained what happened, and I didn't care. They turned to me. The side of Daib's face was bruised.

I walked through the doorway.

"Will you listen?" Daib said.

I paused and really thought about it. "I could kill you."

"Not without me killing you."

I glared at him. Was this atonement? He had not changed. "You already tried. When I was nothing. And you failed. You can *never* kill me."

"I was not trying to kill you," he said. "I was trying to impregnate you."

"All this time, and you don't understand death," I said. "You don't even understand life."

This gave him pause. He pursed his lips and said nothing. I stepped back from him. "I will listen to you . . . until I'm done listening."

"Walk with me," he said. When I did not move, he sighed and added, "I beg you."

I looked at Aro, then at Sola. Neither of them said anything and their faces were wholly unreadable. This was *my* choice.

"Why should I have to choose?" I snapped at them. "I don't want that option. I don't deserve that."

"You deserve freedom," Aro said.

Daib was already walking into the desert.

"You can always just kill him and be done with

it," Sola said. "The only reason I let him live is because he is yours to deal with, not mine."

I stood there for another moment. I hated that I was wearing a dress. I hated how light it was. I undid my large braid and shook out my bushy black hair. I walked into the desert, as dusk faded to night.

We walked for several minutes, scaling the largest sand dune behind Aro's hut. Soon, it was just Daib and me, the hut no longer in sight. I wasn't afraid. I was a sorceress now. I knew five ways I could kill him, and I did not care if he killed me afterward. We walked down a sand dune and there he stopped and turned to me. He looked like he was on fire. Then his entire body changed. Not in spirit; he changed physically. Kponyungo! In the physical world. How?!

I'd made a mistake. This man was more powerful than he'd ever been. I sprang from my body so quickly and became the kponyungo that my physical body collapsed right there in the sand. I met him in the sky like this. He saw me, and he immediately flew back. He was afraid. The spirit is more powerful than the flesh.

"You've become," he said.

He floated to the ground where he changed back to his human self. I returned to my body and stood up. Neither of us let go of our glow. Spirit and Body. "Atone," I growled.

CHAPTER 13

Amends

I listened and throughout his telling, I was aware of who I was talking to and what he had done. My child would have just slaughtered him. But my child was not with me, and my child had saved the world and made it into a new one. Maybe in this one she would have listened . . . and then killed him. I listened, while thinking about killing him. So maybe my recounting of his words are flawed. But I will try to tell you what this man said.

I have come a long way.

Everything has changed. Including me. She left me for dead in my burning office building after her Mwita had slapped an ibibi written in nsibidi script on me. I would have burned that day, but I managed to isolate it and change into a bat. I flew from there seconds before the flames took me. But Mwita's juju took the use of my right leg, my ability to see color and work the Mystic Points. I was a sorcerer who could not be a sorcerer. As I watched them execute your daughter . . . my daughter, I envied her. There are things worse than death.

You look at me as if you want to kill me now. I understand. I have come a long way. Please, let me talk, then you decide. It is just us out here and this is how I want it to be. I know that you are the finest student Aro has ever taught, that Sola has ever seen. But you are not invincible. Not yet. Let me speak and then you decide how you want this to end.

I watched her executed. I enjoyed it. I was sure. I was ready. I would lead my armies. I still had thousands of soldiers loyal to me throughout the Seven Rivers Kingdom. But then Onyesonwu . . . acted. The peacock. Do you know the juju? Has Aro taught it to you? He has. Well, that is what your child used. The peacock—argument, dispute, take action. I didn't know it at the time, but she'd already done it, she'd rewritten the Great Book. The wave simply had not reached where I was. It was already coming. So she'd already won. But she took it further. She saved herself. She saved her Mwita. Maybe she even saved the other girl who'd been with her who had been torn apart.

Time is strange. I cannot describe the Change. It washed over me and I was aware of it. Unlike most, I not only felt it and remember how things were before, I remember how everything changing felt, how I felt. I could feel everything rearranging. And suddenly, I was different, too. I was no longer General Daib. The poison that was in me drained away, Najeeba. You look at me strangely, but it's true. I could feel it.

The things I'd planned to do, for the reasons I had to do them, I felt none of it anymore. I could feel my past changing. My mother was still Bisi and she was still who she was. But it was I who changed. But I remember. I suddenly wasn't where I had been. I was in my office, but it was outside of the Seven Rivers Kingdom. A stone building outside of a small village, where people came to me when they needed my help. A sorcerer's help. I was watering a plant. But I remembered. All of it.

I walked around, trying to understand myself and this new world. For years. I was healed. I could practice the Mystic Points. I still cannot see color in my left eye, but I can in my right. The sorcerer's atonement, it is powerful juju. Did Onyesonwu call it into being as she changed everything? Or was it called by something harder to explain? It settles upon you like a creature. It sits on your shoulders. I would go flying, but I found no peace. I tried to meditate,

I could not be still. I was tormented by who I had been and the juju.

My home was comfortable. I was a powerful and respected sorcerer in my village. People came from other villages, even Seven Rivers to ask for my services. Nuru and Okeke. I even had mistresses whom I enjoyed and who loved me. I should have been content. But I did what so many have been doing. One day, I just decided. I left. But unlike most, I knew where I was going to go. I knew deep in my heart, though everything in my heart resisted it, that I could track you. And I already knew the name Jwahir.

A sorcerer's atonement requires the journey to atonement to be made on foot. At no point can one ride a camel, a scooter, any type of vehicle. And those who can change form cannot do so for faster travel. You must carry all your belongings on your own back. You must travel alone. You are to use this time to see, to grow, to hone who you will become. To prepare and be able to be forgiven.

Those under a sorcerer's atonement who merely must journey to the next house, the next town, close, they still have to work and unburden and face, but they are lucky. For me, I had very far to go. You made the journey on foot with a small child. I do not know how you managed. No preparation, no money, without a clear mind. It is unbelievable. I began my journey understanding I was simply going to my death. A sorcerer's atonement is strong. It set-tles in your chest. It attaches itself to everything that you have. It weaves into your story.

I began my journey West in a rage. I carried a back-pack with a capture station, some food, a foldable tent, my portable, some bushcraft tools, all the things I needed. I did not need much. I was able- bodied now. I was powerful. The juju did not mean I could not practice sorcery. But I was still angry. I had done nothing. But I had; *I remem-bered. It felt unfair. It got in the way of my life.*

At first, I tried to make impossible time. Walking and walking day and well into the night. But soon I grew ex-hausted. And I began to understand that the way was very far and it was over treacherous dead lands. It was not about speed, it was about endurance. I used my portable for its maps, spending days and sometimes weeks in the vil-lages and towns I came across. The people . . . I began to see fewer and fewer Nuru and more and more Okeke as I left Seven Rivers behind.

I gradually learned how to survive in the desert, as well. I'd camp during the day and use my capture station at the height of the day to cool things down and then cool myself more with water. You laugh and I understand. But this was me. I used juju to find plants and creatures to eat. I healed myself when I got sick. And when I camped, I would change into a hawk or a scarab beetle and go flying. I meditated. I came to see that I had been what I now never had been. The murder, genocide, rape, and the fire I'd ignited in so many others, how close I had come to ending an entire people. My thirst for power, dominance, the surety of my superiority and entitlement.

Four years. I have been traveling on foot to atone for four years. Najeeba. Najeeba. Najeeba. Yes, I know your name. I will speak her name, too, Onyesonwu. Onyesonwu. Onyesonwu. I can't go on until I have faced you. Atoned to you. Najeeba. Now a sorceress in her own right. The Kponyungo Sorceress.

———

His light brown eyes glowed in the sunshine. I shut my eyes and slowly shook my head. This man. He had killed me. And here I was standing alone with him in the silence of the desert. What kind of world was this? I opened my eyes and looked right into his. "You are not ready to be forgiven," I growled.

He glared back at me and then looked away. "No. No, I am not." He brought up his hand and pressed it to his face. He squeezed. "I don't know . . . what is wrong with me, what is in me." He suddenly looked deep into my eyes.

I stepped back, afraid.

"I still *hate* you," he said. "I hate your kind. I feel it in my bones. I know I did what I did to you. But I am not *him* anymore. I know why it was wrong, nasty, deeply *sick*, but it's still IN me!"

I shivered. I understood this deeply.

He stepped back and looked at me, earnest. We had the same thought at the same time. I nodded as he said, "There may be a way . . . except, I will never ever trust you."

He reached into the pocket of his pants and brought out a twine of palm fiber. He stretched it, blew hard on it, and then held it out to me. "You have to tie it."

I tied the twine around his wrists and pulled the string tightly, making sure to wet it with my saliva, the only way the juju would work. The twine wound itself snugly around his wrists. Until I touched it, it would never allow him the use of his hands. He sat down hard on the sand, and I walked away from him. I walked up a nearby sand dune and down the side of it. I paused and decided to go over a second one. On the bottom of it, in the soft sand, near a cluster of bushes, I sat down. I took a moment to inspect the bush for snakes, scorpions, and tarantulas. Then I relaxed and shut my eyes.

I stood up in my periwinkle garments. Slowly, I walked back to Daib. I stood over him, looking down. He was looking in the direction I'd gone. He could not see me. He could change physically into a kponyungo, but he did not have my ability to leave. I knelt before him and gazed into his face, bringing my face less than an inch from his.

"Where are you?" I whispered. "Come on." I snarled. "Where. Are. You?" Then . . . I *saw* him. I thrust my spirit hand right into his head. I grasped. Oh, evil thing. A brown wet, coiling, roiling, fibrous thing. It was strong. But I was stronger, and I yanked it out of him. "Foul thing. Evil thing," I said. I pulled and pulled the root from him, flames burning the sand, burning beneath my feet. It fought me, but I held steady. When I was what looked like yards from Daib, the thing thick as his body, it finally let go of Daib and slapped to the sand.

He seemed to see it now, for he shuddered in revulsion and got to his feet. I did not let go. But I changed into the kponyungo and, holding the vile thing in my jaw, I took off with it. I held it as I began to whirl and whirl, sweeping up billows of sand and dust. The thing I held in my mouth shrieked, and I held it tighter. *Fight hard*, I thought. *And now die!* I flew upward. Higher and higher, until I was beyond the stratosphere. It was no longer fighting me now. I flew over the Earth's blue oceans and there I let it plummet, weakly undulating as it fell. I watched it until I could see it no more. And then I flew back to myself.

When I opened my eyes, I sat there for a while. Disgusted. *That* had been living in him. That ugliness. That vileness. That depravity. Alive and strong. I shuttered. I drew the calabash symbol in the sand and plunged my hands into it. I dumped sand over my head like water. Then I performed the cleansing ritual another three times. By the third time, when I finished, I saw Daib coming over the sand dune. I got up.

When he reached me, he dropped to his knees, tears streaming down his face. "It is gone," he said between sobs. "It's *gone!*"

I sighed, looking away. It was hard. Even if I had uprooted it from him and killed it. He still had the same face, the same eyes. I am still a human being. Some things are not forgivable. "Do you remember?" I asked, coldly.

"All of it."

"That is your atonement, then," I said.

He nodded. After a moment he said, "You're powerful."

I sighed. "I've come a long way. What will you do now?"

"I don't know. I have not thought that far."

"You came to me to die."

He laughed.

He doesn't fear death, I thought.

"What of you?" he asked.

"I don't want to talk about that."

He cocked his head, a dark look passing across his face. I had cured him, but there was still something hard in this man. There always would be. I stepped back.

"What did you see?" he asked.

"What do you mean?"

"When you were initiated. We all see it. I have seen it."

I thought about the woman whose death I'd seen. I shivered. The masquerade still haunted me sometimes in my sleep. It was not a good way to die. "Why?" I asked.

He smiled sadly. "Ah, you don't know, then."

"What did *you* see?"

"I saw an old man on a camel surrounded by wild women struck by lightning." He laughed at this as if the thought tickled him.

"And you could feel it, you died with the man?"

"I felt it as if it were my own death," he said. He smirked, as he walked past me. I didn't follow. I closed my eyes, instead. There was something. I frowned, staring at the red of my eyelids in the sun. The woman I'd seen had been in that place, and then the masquerade was above her, unfolding, and unfolding. I didn't visit the memory much because it always made me feel ill. There was something, though. I grunted, stumbling back as if an object had physically hit me. I heard Daib laughing, now yards away. "Ah, now she understands," he said, as he laughed more roughly.

I sat down right there on the sand. Staring up at the sand dune. "How?" I asked. I didn't know. Not yet. I would. Everyone dies. And I knew how I would. And it was awful. I whimpered. "Embrace it," Daib shouted back. "It is yours and yours alone!"

I cursed. Then minutes later, I got up. I dusted

myself off. I wouldn't die out there. That I knew. I walked back to Aro's. I kept watching the sky to see if a bird would fly over my head to arrive there before me. None did. He would walk back. He had truly atoned.

"Did you kill him?" Sola asked.

I smiled, pleased that he thought it possible. So he did not think I was so soft.

"She did not kill him," Aro said. "And that is good."

I went home. As I cooked a large dinner for myself, I felt it. I was glad I had not killed him, too. Even if Daib had known I wouldn't.

CHAPTER 14

Dead Juju

"This juju is for bringing water. It will not work," Aro said. "It is one of those made for the times before these times. Back before what you saw the day you looked into the water. Nevertheless, it's good to work on jujus that have died, so you know what absolute failure feels like."

I was still disappointed. I'd read the stories about it in a book from the House of Osugbo. I'd followed all the instructions perfectly. I fasted for days to increase my focus and strength. Even Sola, who'd stopped by to check on me, had told me it had not worked since before the Phoenix made the lands desert, over 500 years ago. I wasn't so arrogant to think that I'd succeed . . . but I was a little. I'd hoped. I guess that was the lesson Aro wanted me to learn, the bitterness Aro wanted me to taste. I'd had so much success with almost everything else, even though I suffered consequences. I rolled onto my back and stared into the darkening sky, my lips so dry that I could feel them beginning to crack.

"Go home and cook a meal," Aro said, getting up, laughing. "It's not happening today."

"Maybe I'll just sleep here," I groaned. "I don't think I can get up."

"Do whatever you like," he said. "But do not stay too long. You are dehydrated."

For an hour, I lay there, watching the sun set. I thought about the last time I'd lain on the bare sand for hours like this, but, for once, the memory didn't attach to the moment. Instead, I noted it and moved on to contemplating the clear sky. Not a cloud in it. When I nearly rose from my body as the kponyungo, I sat up. This was not the time or the place. I considered going to Dedan's and then felt annoyed. He had gone to see his parents in Banza for a week. I walked back to Aro's hut.

I was there for a few hours, when I heard the first rumble of thunder. I was poring over the books I'd brought from the House of Osugbo, particularly the one about wildlife of the Seven Rivers. I was so focused on what I was reading, that I didn't notice the sun get blocked out by giant clouds. When I heard the rumble, I thought I'd imagined it. I hadn't given up on the juju working, if I were to be honest. I'd dreamed of rain and woken up just before sunrise with a weird tingling in the bottoms of my feet and an ache in my joints. When I'd looked at the sky, it had been cloudless. Dry. I let it go . . . but I'd still hoped.

The rumble of thunder came again. This time, louder. I grinned big. Then I looked up and saw the darkness. I dropped my book and ran outside. The sky was churning and roiling. I screamed with joy. "ARO!!! ARO!!!!!" I ran to his hut. He was already standing outside in the back, looking at the sky.

"What have you done, woman?" he asked, but he looked mystified.

"You think this was all me?"

"Of course."

"But I only called a *few* clouds!"

"You're inner voice apparently is much louder than your physical one." He turned and swept past me.

"Where are you going?!"

"The House of Osugbo. There may be something I can do."

"What about me?"

"Go home . . . prepare. A lot is coming." Then he was striding up the path, past his cactus gate.

I only knew a few repelling charms and jujus. I used them to keep sand out of my home and to protect my garden from harsh winds. It took some thought to tweak them for repelling water. Rain was a rare blessing, always. When it began to fall, people ran outside, no matter what they were wearing. It felt strange to do what I was doing. I considered going to the Ada and some of my neighbors and doing the same. However, most already saw me as strange, I didn't think I could answer all their questions.

Still, by this time, people had come out into the road to talk about, point and stare at the sky. Everyone was on edge.

"I have never seen the sky look like that."

"My home has been in the family for generations, I hope it can handle this."

"The rainmaker is saying this is unprecedented."

I listened to everyone and said nothing. I felt so guilty. I had called for a few clouds, imagining the type that was so full of moisture, capture stations couldn't make it disappear. Maybe that had been a little much. Maybe it is best to ask for what you need, instead of an exaggeration of it because you don't think the juju will work. My lack of confidence in the Mystic Points had caused this. It didn't matter that it had not worked for Aro, Sola or anyone. The lesson was that I was still to respect it. In the right hands, it would work. My hands had been right.

There was a rumble of thunder from far away, and we all fell silent. I resisted the strong urge to tell everyone to come to my house. I wasn't sure if the house would hold up under all the water, but I felt it had the best chance. Nevertheless, I also knew that I had to keep quiet. Times had changed, but I still sensed an undercurrent of suspicion when it came to me. It was as if I still carried the scent of the Before and of who I was in that time. I went home and, as I shut the door, the guilt pressed down more heavily on my shoulders, along with the dryness in my throat.

The rain arrived an hour later.

"Ani is testing me," I muttered.

The rain came down heavily all that day and, at some point, the power went off. The lightning was so bright that I could see it when I closed my eyes and the thunder was so loud that I could feel the noise in my chest. There was a great crash followed by screams and shouts. I ran outside and saw my neighbor's house had been struck. No one was hurt and the fire was quickly stanched by the rain. More water fell from the sky.

When it grew late, I don't know how I was able to sleep, but I did. Hours later, I jumped from bed when I heard something that sounded like the land moaning. I put on the blue dress that I had set aside for when things got bad. It was close fitting and I moved smoothly in it. Outside was dark, it being many hours before daybreak. All seemed normal in my house. I went outside. I froze. The road had become a raging river. As I stared, the water carried a struggling camel by. Yes, he could swim. No, swimming didn't save him.

Several of the houses were already slightly flooded, the occupants using buckets to throw out water. Despite the chaos, several people just stood there in awe. I looked down. The river of water bent away from the threshold of my house. But what of when the water rose? The wind had also picked up. *Waves*, I thought. *I didn't think of waves.*

"Do you need help?" I shouted across the road to one of the neighbors.

"We'll be okay," she shouted back. "For now."

By sunrise, Jwahir was a different place. For miles, all was water. Whatever was in its way was saturated or swept away. The basin shape of Jwahir's layout contained it perfectly. As the water rose, people were also forced to rise. Most of the homes in Jwahir were one story, so this meant that most people were on their roofs.

What happened in my house was most bizarre. My charm worked . . . well. As the water rose, it was as if there was a barrier around my house and my garden that repelled the water. All I could think of were my neighbors whom I'd basically betrayed by not protecting their homes out of fear of suspicion. What would people think when they saw my house now? I couldn't think about that at the moment. This was a desert town; it couldn't understand so much water, people didn't know how to swim . . . and I had caused this!

I could see the road through the window. Underwater, the view was clear in some places. But in others, sand was whipped about by the current. My garden was in a giant air bubble.

Though it was still raining, the sun peaked through the clouds once in a while, shining rays of light through the water. It was lovely. *And Jwahir was drowning in this loveliness*, I thought. Getting out of the house was tricky. I went to the back door. Slowly, I slid it open and stepped into my garden. About two feet above my head was the wall of water. Again, I wondered what people would think when they saw this.

I walked to the farthest part of the garden and stepped up to the wall of water. Gently, I reached forward and touched it. It rippled, but the force held. I poked a finger through it. Then my whole arm. I pulled it out. My arm was soaked, the water dribbling downward and then quickly evaporating.

"All right," I whispered.

I had swum once, decades ago, when I was with Idris. A neighbor had filled a giant tub with water to irrigate his corn farm. A large cloud had been passing by and he'd taken advantage of it, using all five of his capture stations. Most villagers were afraid to try swimming in it. I was one of two brave enough. The other was an old woman who'd fled the Seven Rivers Kingdom years ago; she'd grown up swimming in the rivers. Everyone had oohed and aahed as she swam, including my neighbor. When it was my turn, I just imagined what it was like to fly as the kponyungo and swimming came naturally to me.

I relied on this feeling now as I first pushed one arm through the wall of water and then the other. I pulled them out. I took in a deep breath and then dove in. As soon as I was through the barrier, I reoriented myself. I swam upward, feeling awkward and strange at first. Then I made friends with the water. It was like heavy, slow wind that I could not breathe.

I swam easily to the surface, waded to the house across from me and climbed onto a roof. There were people standing on the other side, but with all the rain still falling, no one noticed me.

"Najeeba!" my neighbor Polo called from his roof a house away. "How are you doing?"

"I'm okay, for now. Where is your wife?"

"On the other side," he said. "I think this is going to get worse."

"You think so, Polo?"

"We have to be ready if it does."

"What should we do?" I asked.

"You can swim well . . . can you make it over here? I'm calling all the men to decide on a plan."

I jumped into the water. I could have protected everyone's house, I could have said it was Aro who'd done it. Why hadn't I thought of this solution before? The last thing I needed was for someone to jump in that water who was a worse swimmer than me. They'd drown. The current of water rushing between my home and Polo's was remarkably warm, and I was reminded of the vein of a great beast. The current would change any moment. I needed to move faster. The water changed direction and swirled me away from Polo's house.

"Someone get her!" a woman shouted. "She'll drown!"

"So will anyone who goes after her," a man said.

The water swept me northwest and then up against another neighbor's house. I clung to the roof and a young man named Adama ran over and grabbed my arm. He hauled me out of the water onto their roof. Not far from me, the water had swirled into a small whirlpool; it would have pulled me down.

"Are you all right?" Adama asked. He looked terrified.

I nodded, putting my arms around my chest. My dress was soaked and one could easily see through it.

"Thank you," I said.

"I can't swim. Not at all," he blurted.

"Well, thank goodness you didn't have to," I said.

I had only swum about a quarter of the way to Polo's house. The water was too strong.

"Hopefully, all this will pass soon," Adama said. His wife and three young children came to sit with me and this act of kindness made me want to cry more. I could have protected them better.

I looked at my hands, my helpless hands that were now capable of so much after years of training. I frowned, holding them closer to my face to make sure I was seeing what I was seeing. I touched the thin brown webbing that had started to grow between my fingers. When I touched it, I could feel it. I knew if I cut it, that it would hurt and bleed. I could even see tiny veins snaking through the flesh. I stretched my legs before me. My toes were starting to web, too. *But I'm not Eshu*, I thought. *Am I?* I could witch, I could become the kponyungo, and I could project my spirit. I had never been able to change my physical body; these were abilities of Aro and my daughter Onyesonwu.

Someone nearby shouted, and then suddenly many were shouting. Polo's house. Something was happening on the other side of it. There was a roaring sound now that drowned out everyone's voice. A woman screamed, "The water is alive! AHHHH, Kadidia!!"

No time to question what had happened to me. I got up and, to the family's surprise, dove into the water. I ignored my fear as much as I could, focusing on my destination and making my body able to arrive at it. I didn't pay any attention to the people who shouted at me as I passed their flooded homes. I did not pay attention to the fact that I could barely tell where I was going.

These floods would be talked about for decades. And I swam through it. I grew more confident. I moved faster, easier. And soon, I barely came up for air. This was also something people would talk about. People would say that I had fallen into the water by accident and that was when something bizarre happened to me. Some said that I changed into a giant fish. Others speculated that after I fell in, I got up and ran on top of the water.

I reached Polo's house just in time to hear a girl's screams grow loud and then diminish. Then the roaring of the water sharpened into a sucking sound as I scrambled onto the roof, disregarding my fatigue. I'd only had to climb up about a foot and half.

"Papa! You can't!" a woman screamed. She was on her belly, holding a hand out. Below her, a man in the water, was holding on for dear life with one hand and reaching for a camel with the other—a camel who was being carried toward him by the strength of the maelstrom in the water! The whirlpool that had appeared where the camel stables should have been. A vortex of water that was the color of wet sand. The sand must have been caving in underneath. *What kind of horror is this*? I thought *My fault!*

"Forget the camel!" someone else yelled. "It's lost."

"I grab the camel, then Kadidia can grab on to it!" he shouted. "Otherwise, she'll be too far!"

"Papa!!!" Kadidia was screaming as she came back around. She was moving dangerously close to the center of the funnel where she'd be sucked down.

Vaguely aware of my webbed and elongated feet as they slapped on the roof's surface, I dove in. The maelstrom took me right away but I saw Kadidia and managed to grab her arm. Then I fought. Sandy water whipped past me into the whirlpool. The suction pulled at my body and I could feel my kneecaps, hip joints and spine separating. I fought harder. My hand cramped and I could feel my grip on the girl slipping.

I looked back for moment as I grabbed and grabbed perpendicular to the current. It was like an underwater witch. One who would tear us apart in seconds. I glanced at the girl's face. Her eyes were bulging, staring back at me, her breath held, but not for much longer. Soon we'd both drown.

The water was strong, destructive, and relentless, but it also had mercy. I felt it let go. And when it did, we shot forward. When our heads came above water, I heard roars and shouts of relief. I paddled to Polo's roof, as the whirlpool behind us began to dissipate, and we were pulled out of the water.

Someone's rapa was thrown over my shoulders. I was thankful because it covered my elongated webbed feet and hands. No one saw that my arms were a bit too long and my legs were a bit too muscular. No one asked why I didn't vomit water and sand, like the girl. There was too much joy, too much relief.

I stayed the night with everyone on Polo's roof. There had to be at least ten of us up there. Huddled in the center of the roof, as far as we could get form the water. The rain stopped by nightfall and the water began quickly diminishing by the next day. The desert drank up the water in great gulps. By afternoon, I could walk home. My shop was gutted, but it would not be difficult to rebuild. The blacksmithing shop was made of stone, so though the ironware and equipment inside was washed into a corner and the fire in the bellows was put out, it was otherwise intact. And my house was spared, but the same couldn't be said for everyone else's. All the other homes had been under water. A few homes even collapsed completely.

By the evening, Dedan returned. We hugged for well over five minutes in front of my house. "Is it wrong of me to have been certain that you'd be all right?" he said into my ear. "Both you and the House of Osugbo?"

I felt yet another pang of guilt. The storm I'd called up had hit more than just Jwahir. It had truly been huge and unprecedented. Even soaking the town of Banza.

"You're a hero," Dedan added.

I let go of him. "You've already heard? I was looking forward to telling you all about it."

"That kind of news travels fast, sorceress. The girl you saved has been speaking about you like you're some character in the Great Book." I let him pull me to him. He slipped an arm around my waist, ran a hand over my belly and slid it down further. I sighed, feeling all my stress leave me. "You're okay," he said.

"I'm okay," I breathed.

"What you did will be good for business."

"Very."

He led me to the bedroom, and I thought about what Aro had said about being reckless. For two hours, we were reckless.

═══════

When I went to the Ada's house, I found her in a heartbroken bundle on the floor.

There were three men who had stayed with her during the storm. They'd had to escape onto make-shift rafts as her house was submerged. However, when it was all over, none of them quite knew how to handle her grief when she saw what was left of the gorgeous and extensive mural she'd painted on her walls. They'd offered her tea, kind words, and hugs and still she cried. Days after the storm, I knew that all I could do was hold her.

"It was meant to be underwater, don't you think?" I whispered into her ear as she sobbed. Even the old fish man she'd spent the most time on had swum away, that part of the mural sloughing off entirely and floating out of the house. When the rain had started falling heavily, Aro had offered to protect her home and the Ada had refused. I don't exactly know why. Had they fought? Did she not want to explain to others why her home was untouched? I knew it was the type of thing I could not ask her about. Aro's huts were fine, as I knew they would be.

"The land has changed," he said. "I think the

rains are returning. This is why the charm worked so well."

"Do you think the desert will begin to turn green again?"

"We will see," he said.

CHAPTER 15

One Way Witch

By the end of the week, Jwahir was full of butterflies. Large orange creatures with graceful black antennae. They fluttered lazily about, bringing squeals of joy from children, giggles from women, and a sense of something coming for men. For me, I knew it was an omen. I woke up that morning with one strange phrase on my mind, and I didn't know what it meant . . . but I did. "One Way Witch." There truly was only one way. I had known from the moment I met with Aro.

"The coming of the butterflies. Rarely is it clearer when a student is a master," Aro said.

I nodded. Because I knew. "You nearly drowned Jwahir, yet you're so full of wisdom now." He paused at this and then continued. "Things will keep germinating and manifesting within you. Answers will appear to you before the questions. Like how were you able to change your body when you are not Eshu."

The floods had not just happened in Jwahir, the rain hit even as far as Banza. Dedan believed that it may have gone even further. I hadn't dared to fly out and look. He and most of the residents of Banza had fled up the hill where the town's twins used to reside. The twins on the hill had been a protective force for the town when both were alive and the hill maintained that mythology. Thankfully, for in this way, no one in Banza had died.

"We watched the storm happen from way up there. It was eerie because the entire sky was churning. From horizon to horizon. Then when the sun set, you could see all the lightning as it rained. When the sun came up . . . I now know what the sea must look like!"

I nodded but didn't say much else. I couldn't bring myself to tell him that I had caused the whole thing. "I'm glad you're okay," I said. "I'm glad everyone is."

"My home isn't," he said. His home had been completely underwater. His neighbors had known that he traveled, and they'd done all they could to clear it out and clean it up, but this only meant that he returned to a clean, but mostly empty home. Most of the furniture and decorations he had were glass, and they survived but not much else. "But I didn't have much anyway," he said. "Haven't even checked on my shop."

"I . . . I have to tell you something." I was standing in front of Njeri's portrait and it gave me strength to have her looking on behind me.

"What now?" he breathed, resting his head on my couches cushion.

"You remember what I told you? About why I became Aro's student?"

"Yeah, you said that someone, usually a parent or older relative, blood, has to ask for someone to be a sorcerer for them to become one. For you, it was your father, right?"

"Yes."

"And that in the Before, the Nuru were racist and . . . committing genocide." He frowned and paused.

"Don't let your mind go there," I said.

He shook his head. "No, I will. I have to keep going there. It's the only way. I have to go *through* it. So, the Nuru were racist . . . they claimed it was all in the Great Book, but anyone with a brain would know that that Book was poisoning them. Anyway, your father's family . . . right, your father's family was wiped out because his sister and a Nuru boy fell in love. The boy's family killed the boy and then came and killed your father's sister, the entire family except for him and he fled as a child. But there was more . . ." He slapped at his temples. "Ugh, so ugly, Najeeba. The Before was toxic."

I nodded, but I didn't interrupt him.

"In your village, where you grew up, even though things were actually okay, there was something there, something . . ."

"Something haunted my village," I said. I shivered. I didn't speak of it much, though I thought about it often. Mostly when I was the kponyungo, and I felt powerful and beyond death. "It's called the Cleanser and it's still there."

"How do you know?"

"I saw it." And I knew this day would come. "And I'm going to kill it."

Dedan didn't flinch at my word. "I will go with you."

I blinked. "No. I do this alone. It's my wrong to right."

"It's not yours," he said. "You didn't create the thing. And you won't do it alone. I'm coming with you."

I tried to speak but no words came. It was as if he'd worked some sort of juju on me. Aro had said he was sensitive, and who knew what Aro had been secretly teaching him without my knowing. It had crossed my mind more than once that Aro had been teaching Dedan just to annoy me. "I will go with you. My shop can run on its own, if it's still even there, and my home is ruined."

"Dedan, I don't know—"

"I am coming with you," he said again.

We went to Aro and Aro said we should leave right away. "When it is time, then there's no time to waste," he said.

The day before we set out, I walked with Aro to the remains of the glass house. People still came to this place, some to pray and some to just stare at the ruins that hadn't been washed away. It was surprising just how much of the glass was still there. We stood on a sand dune looking down at it. "Your Dedan has given Jwahir something that will help it relieve some of its tension."

"People still talk about the day he destroyed it," I said.

"There is a painter going around selling paintings

of him destroying it, and there is a poet who has written a whole book of poetry about it and what it all means. Soon they will teach about it in the schools." Aro nodded to himself, pleased. "It will be good for him to leave, too."

"He will never find answers to his questions," I said. "They are from a different time that no longer exists."

Aro nodded. "But he may find better questions. And there is one other reason that I think it is good for him to go with you."

"What is that?" I asked.

"You know."

I did.